"A labor which might have made Hercules pause is persuading a publisher to issue a collection of short stories. At the first suggestion of it they whine, whimper, climb trees, and go seek their home in the rocks like the aunts—or is it the conies? As I have somehow managed to do this three times—once with an agent's assistance, once against an agent's active indifference, and once by the underhanded method of promising and actually delivering a novel as sweetener—I feel wise and ripe with wisdom beyond my many years and compelled to impart some of it to my readers. . . ."

—Avram Davidson, *Preface*

"A teller of tales . . . I can imagine nothing better than taking a long train journey, oh, let us say, on the old Orient Express with good food and good wine waiting in the diner, and seated across from me, the personification of their books, such as Mr. Kipling, Saki, Collier, Chesterton, and, holding his own, amid them all, Avram Davidson in high good humor."

—Ray Bradbury, *Introduction*

STRANGE SEAS AND SHORES

Avram Davidson

SF
ace books

A Division of Charter Communications Inc.
A GROSSET & DUNLAP COMPANY
51 Madison Avenue
New York, New York 10010

STRANGE SEAS AND SHORES
copyright© 1971 by Avram Davidson

An ACE Book

First Ace printing: August 1981
Published Simultaneously in Canada
2 4 6 8 0 9 7 5 3 1
Manufactured in the United States of America

ACKNOWLEDGEMENTS:

"Sacheverell," copyright ©1964 by Mercury Press, Inc. *The Magazine of Fantasy and Science Fiction*, March 1964.

"Take Wooden Indians," copyright ©1959 by Galaxy Publishing Corporation. *Galaxy*, June 1959.

"The Vat," copyright ©1961 by Mercury Press, Inc. *The Magazine of Fantasy and Science Fiction*, October 1961.

"The Tail-Tied Kings," copyright ©1962 by Galaxy Publishing Corporation, *Galaxy*, April 1962.

"Paramount Ulj," copyright ©1958 by Galaxy Publishing Corporation. *Galaxy*, October 1958.

"A Bottle Full of Kismet," copyright © 1971 by Avram Davidson.

"The Goobers," copyright © 1965 by Magnum-Royal Publications Inc. *Swank*, November 1965.

"Dr. Morris Goldpepper Returns," copyright © 1962 by Galaxy Publishing Corporation. *Galaxy*, December 1962.

"The Certificate," copyright © 1959 by Mercury Press, Inc. *The Magazine of Fantasy and Science Fiction*, March 1959.

"Ogre in the Vly," copyright © 1959 by Digest Productions, Inc. *IF*, July 1959.

"Après Nous," copyright © 1960 by Mercury Press, Inc. *The Magazine of Fantasy and Science Fiction*, March 1960.

"Climacteric," copyright ©1960 by Mercury Press, Inc. *The Magazine of Fantasy and Science Fiction*, August 1960.

"Yo-Ho and Up," copyright ©1960 by Mercury Press, Inc. *The Magazine of Fantasy and Science Fiction*, December 1960.

"The Sixty-Third Street Station," copyright ©1962 by Mercury Press, Inc. *The Magazine of Fantasy and Science Fiction*, March 1962.

"The House the Blakeneys Built," copyright ©1964 by Mercury Press, Inc. *The Magazine of Fantasy and Science Fiction*, January 1965.

"The Power of Every Root," copyright © 1967 by Mercury Press Inc. *The Magazine of Fantasy and Science Fiction*, October 1967.

"The Sources of the Nile," copyright © 1960 by Mercury Press, Inc. *The Magazine of Fantasy and Science Fiction*, January 1961.

Contents

Preface

A labor which might have made Hercules pause is persuading a publisher to issue a collection of short stories.
At the first suggestion of it they whine, whimper, climb
trees, and go seek their home in the rocks like the aunts
—or is it the conies? As I have somehow managed to do
this three times—once with an agent's assistance, once
against an agent's active indifference, and once by the
underhanded method of promising and actually delivering a novel as sweetener—I feel wise and ripe with wisdom beyond my many years and compelled to impart
some of it to my readers.

When I first thought of such a collection I had never
had a book published at all, and very little of anything
else, and I wrapped the typescripts of all my short
stories (few of which had ever been subjected to a jus
primus noctae or droit de seigneur or Library of Congress
copyright) in an old raincoat and, letting the weather
beat upon my more expendable integuments, took the
whole lot to be seen by Miss Judith Merril, who had already begun her career as a writer and an anthologist of
note and merit.

"I call them *Tales of the Old and the Curious*," I said,
"and I did send them to an agent, but he sent them
right back." —He later made a spectacular failure, too,
and was last heard of in the Andaman Islands, or somewhere, as a beachcomber in a small way of business.
—Miss Merril, having read them, smiled at me indul-
gently and said that publishers *hated* to print collections

of short stories and that I was really an essayist and the opportunities for essayists were about the same as they were for buggy-whip tasselers. She next caused me to levitate by announcing her plans to reprint one of my tales, but this did not seem to satisfy her.

"What can I do to help you?" she asked, more of herself than of me. "I can introduce you to a magazine editor," she said. I said, "Wow!" "He may not buy anything," she forewarned me, "but he'll give you a drink." WellSir and MemSir, he *did* give me a drink. (Was it Petrarch, who said, "I would rather decline six nouns than one drink"?)

And he bought my sweet lavendar, too, I mean my stories, I mean some of them. That was Robert P. Mills, then Managing Editor of *The Magazine of Fantasy and Science Fiction* and *Ellery Queen's Mystery Magazine*. "Have you ever thought of submitting anything to our other magazine as well?" he asked. I said, "I've never written a regular detective story." "It is sufficient," he said, "if the story contains some element of crime." "It is sufficient," murmured Miss Merril, "if one of the characters beats his wife."

"Well, it just so happens that I have with me," I said, fumbling in my ditty-bag with fevered nonchalance, because it *did* just happen that— And, "I've often read that phrase," said Mr. Mills, bemused, "but this is the first time I've ever actually heard it spoken." Nevertheless, that one he didn't buy, nobody ever bought it, and for all I know it was used to start fires by the housemaid of John Stuart Mill after she ran out of the manuscript of Carlyle's *French Revolution*, which she had previously used for the purpose. Miss Merril, not content by having boosted my career by this introduction and by reprinting my story *The Golem* in her SF annual, next proceeded to introduce

me to everyone in the world of imaginative letters, except
for Herman Melville, who was drunk at the time. He had
written *Moby Dick* for no other purpose than the hopes
of getting that job in the Customs House from the public-
ity, and after that he just didn't *care.*

This brings us to the old question, "Is it What you know
or Who (or Whom) you know?" Let me tell you. It is
both. Out of these kindnesses of Miss Merril's heart blos-
somed many of my stories and books, as well as—indi-
rectly—my first marriage, my first child, and (despite
those same kindnesses) my present position as Grand
Middle-aged Man of Something or Other which even today occasionally gets me invited to attend the coffee break
at a university seminar.

Of course all such traffic occurs on a two-way street.
And, when *I* was first, well not exactly an editor, that
came later, when I was a sort of apprentice assistant
editor, I once encouraged someone who became subse-
quently well-known under his real name of Shimon Win-
celberg as author of television and motion picture and
both Broadway and Off Broadway plays: he in course of
time made me acquainted with Ward Moore, who not
only encouraged me to send to Anthony Boucher the story
which won me Miss Merril's attention but also introduced
me to Ray Bradbury and many years later became god-
father to my son . . . What? No, not Ray Bradbury:
Ward Moore. And if you are by now thoroughly confused
I believe you will be in a fit state and condition to go on
and read the rest of this simply splendid little book.

Night Travel on the Orient Express
Destination: Avram

Introduction by Ray Bradbury

There are several risks connected with writing an Introduction to another writer's works.

One, you may overpraise, in which case the reader turns off, saying: He can't be that good. The reader then approaches all the stories with a chip on his shoulder, daring the writer to be as fine as he has been told.

Two, you may underpraise. In an effort to be fair and unassuming, you may hold back. In which case the reader says: How peculiar. This critic seems dreadfully quiet. The stories that follow, then, can't really be worth while.

And so the book is shut.

I would like to balance myself somewhere between the two extremes. In the case of Avram Davidson, this isn't easy. For I have enjoyed his work for many years now, and feel that he is long overdue for discovery.

Let me plunge right in, then, looking neither to right nor to left, ahead nor behind.

Avram Davidson, to me, combines many talents and attributes, including imagination, style and, perhaps above all, wit.

Many of these stories are complete mysteries, puzzles. Avram Davidson starts us in a fog and lets us orient ourselves slowly. He tosses us bits of information. We do not know where we are, who the characters are, or what they are up to. Slowly we begin to find our way toward the light, with Mr. Davidson always a few quick steps ahead, calling us, as a good storyteller calls: This way, now this, over here, now up, now down, now to one side, come along!

And he knows exactly how much information to give us any one second. He knows how to pay out the rope, inch by inch. Too slow and we would fall asleep. Too fast and we would miss the point. His knack for a proper pace is that of a true teller of tales.

A teller of tales. The designation is almost an insult in our time. We have been sore put upon by your *New Yorker* slice-of-life writer and all of the other non-talents of our age appearing in magazine after magazine, so that when we come upon such as Avram Davidson we go into a mild shock of surprise. For this is what story writing once was, and can be again, if we leave it to more capable hands.

Reading through his collection, a number of storytellers' names leaped to mind. I hope that Mr. Davidson will approve this list that tossed itself up, now here, now there: Rudyard Kipling, Saki, John Collier, G. K. Chesterton.

I could make the list longer, but those must do for now.

I can imagine nothing better than taking a long train journey, oh, let us say, on the old Orient Express with good food and good wine waiting in the diner, and seated across from me, the personification of their books, such as Mr. Kipling, Saki, Collier, Chesterton, and, holding his own, amid them all, Avram Davidson in high good humor.

I realize that is a rare fine company I have put him in, but I have always been one to stick my neck out through affection and admiration. If I would not say he measures completely to their height, I *do* say this: On such a train, on such a sweet night journey, these men would gladly listen to Avram Davidson and read and enjoy him. You would find his stories in their book bags, even as you would find theirs in his. If their abilities differ, as do tastes, we know they are good companions, and similar people who would travel well because of their knack for the agreeably strange, the small truth that becomes a lie or the lie suddenly revealed as truth.

I would gladly ride with these and stay up half the night training across Europe in the dark, and even keep my mouth shut, to hear their tales.

The shadow of Kafka might fall across their night-traveling talk, here or there.

And outside of Budapest, through some whim of impossible geography, Dickens' phantom signalman might flag the train to a ghost stop for some while.

I mention all these people and the vibrations they give off because readers always want to know: Well, what's this new writer like? And you mumble and cudgel your brain and come up with tired labels and lame theories. Avram Davidson is not like any of these, and yet, as I have said, their night company was made for him. They would ask him in out of the corridor, even if he were simply passing, disguised as ticket agent, covered with strange punched-out confetti left over from most peculiar destinations.

There is a bit of the scalawag in Avram Davidson. He can be wrongheaded, but it is the sort of wrongheadedness we did not tolerate in Bernard Shaw so much as delight in. We enjoy an outrageous person, for so many puritan radicals among us wouldn't know how to radicalize a mole, much less outrage a snail. Davidson, no less than John Collier, is a maker of gyroscopes that by their very logic of manufacture *shouldn't* work but—lo! there above the abyss they *do* spin and hum.

I will not, repeat not, select my list of favorites in this book. That sort of thing is mildly ridiculous, for if I like "Sacheverell" you will prefer "The Vat," and if I yell for "The Tail-Tied Kings" you will campaign for "A Bottle

Full of Kismet," whereupon I will shift canvas and put in with you.

A final warning, not repeated often enough: Collections of short stories, like vitamins, should be taken, one or two a night, just before sleep. It will be a temptation, but don't gorge yourself on this book. Easy does it, and much affection for this teller of tales Avram Davidson will be the healthy result.

At the end of a week of such nights, you will have developed a proper appetite for further journeys to that strange, wild country of Avram in all the years ahead.

"More!" will say you.

"More!" will say I.

How can he resist our cries?

> RAY BRADBURY
> Los Angeles, California
> November 18, Apollo Year Two.

STRANGE SEAS AND SHORES

Sacheverell

The front windows of the room were boarded up, and inside it was dark and cold and smelled very bad. There was a stained mattress on which a man wrapped in a blanket lay snoring, a chair with no back; a table which held the remains of a bag of hamburgers, several punched beer cans, and a penny candle which cast shadows all around.

There was a scuffling sound in the shadows, then a tiny rattling chattering noise, then a thin and tiny voice said, tentatively, "You must be very *cold*, George . . ." No reply. "Because I know *I'm* very cold . . ." the voice faded out. After a moment it said, "He's still asleep. A man needs his rest. It's very *hard* . . ." The voice seemed to be listening for something, seemed not to hear it; after an instant, in a different tone, said, "All right."

"*Hmm?*" it asked the silence. The chattering broke out again for just a second, then the voice said, "Good afternoon, Princess. Good afternoon, Madame. And General —how very nice to see *you*. I wish to invite you to a tea-party. We will use the best set of doll dishes and if any-one wishes to partake of something *stronger*, I believe the Professor—" the voice faltered, continued, "—has a drop of oh-be-joyful in a bottle on the sideboard. And now pray take seats."

The wind sounded outside; when it died away, leaving the candleflame dancing, there was a humming noise which rose and fell like a moan, then ended abruptly on a sort of click. The voice resumed, wavering at first, "Coko and Moko? No—I'm very sorry, I really can't invite them, they're very stupid, they don't know how to behave and they can't even talk . . ."

The man on the stained mattress woke in a convulsive movement that brought him sitting up with a cry. He threw his head to the right and left and grimaced and struck at the air.

"Did you have a bad *dream*, George?" the voice asked, uncertainly.

George said, *"Uhn!"* thrusting at his eyes with the cushions of his palms. He dropped his hands, cleared his throat and spat, thickly. Then he reached out and grabbed the slack of a chain lying on the floor, one end fastened to a tableleg, and began to pull it in. The chain resisted, he tugged, something fell and squeaked, and George, continuing to pull, hauled in his prize and seized it.

"Sacheverell—"

"I hope you didn't have a bad *dream*, George—"

"Sacheverell—was anybody here? You lie to me and—"

"No, George, honest! Nobody was here, George!"

"You lie to me and I'll kill you!"

"I wouldn't lie to you, George. I know it's wicked to lie."

George glared at him out of his reddened eyes, took a firmer grip with both hands, and squeezed. Sacheverell cried out, thrust his face at George's wrist. His teeth clicked on air, George released him, abruptly, and he scuttled away. George smeared at his trouser-leg with his sleeve, made a noise of disgust. "Look what you done, you filthy little ape!" he shouted.

Sacheverell whimpered in the shadows. "I can't help it, George. I haven't got any sphincter muscle, and you *scared* me, you *hurt* me . . ."

George groaned, huddled in under his blanket. "A million dollars on the end of this chain," he said; "and Om living in this hole, here. Like a wino, like a smokey, like a *bum!*" He struck the floor with his fist. "It don't make sense!" he cried, shifting around till he was on all fours, then pushing himself erect. Wrapping the blanket around his shoulders, he shambled quickly to the door, checked the bolt, then examined in turn the boarded-up front windows and the catch on the barred and frost-rimmed back window. Then he did something in a corner, cursing and sighing.

Under the table Sacheverell tugged on his chain ineffectually. "I don't *like* it here, George," he said. "It's cold and it's dirty and I'm dirty and cold, too, and I'm hungry. It's all dark here and nobody ever comes here and I don't like it, George, I don't like it here one bit. I wish I was back with the Professor again. I was very *happy* then. The Professor was nice to me and so was the Princess and Madame Opal and the General. They were the only ones in on the secret, until *you* found out."

George swung around and looked at him. One eye sparked in the candle-light.

"We used to have tea-parties and Madame Opal always brought chocolates when she came, even when she came alone, and she read love stories to me out of a magazine book with pictures and they were all true. Why can't I be back with the Professor again?"

George swallowed, and opened his mouth with a little

smacking sound. "Professor Whitman died of a heart-attack," he said.

Sacheverell looked at him, head cocked. "An attack . . ."

"So he's *dead!* So forget about him!" the words tore out of the man's mouth. He padded across the room. Sacheverell retreated to the end of his chain.

"I don't know what the Hell Om gunna *do* . . . In a few weeks now, they'll tear this rotten building down. Maybe," he said, slyly, putting his foot down on the chain, "I'll sell you to a zoo. Where you belong." He bent, grunting, and picked up the chain.

Sacheverell's teeth began to chatter. "I *don't!*" he shrilled. "I *don't* belong in a zoo! The little people they have there are *stu*pid—they don't know how to be*have*, and they can't even *talk!*"

George closed one eye, nodded; slowly, very slowly, drew in the chain. "Come on," he said. "Level with me. Professor Whitman had a nice little act, there. How come he quit and took off and came here?" Slowly he drew in the chain. Sacheverell trembled, but did not resist.

"We were going to go to a laboratory in a college," he said. "He told me. It was a waste to keep me doing silly tricks with Coko and Moko, when I was so smart. He should have done it before, he said."

George's mouth turned up on one side, creasing the stubble. "Naa, Sacheverell," he said. "That don't make sense. You know what they do to monkeys in them labs? They cut 'em up. That's all. I *know*. I went to one and I asked. They pay about fifteen bucks and then they cut 'em up." He made a scissors out of his fingers and went *k'khkhkhkh* . . . Sacheverell shuddered. George set his foot on the chain again and took hold of him by the neck. He poked him in the stomach with his finger,

stiff. It had grown colder, the man's breath shown misty
in the tainted air. He poked again. Sacheverell made a
sick noise, struggled. "Come on," George said. "Level
with me. There's a million dollars inside of you, you
dirty little ape. There's *gotta* be. Only I don't know
how. So you tell me."

Sacheverell whimpered. "I don't *know*, George. I don't
know."

The man scowled, then grinned slyly. "That's what *you*
say. I'm not so sure. You think I don't know that if
They found out, They'd take you away from me? Sure.
A million bucks . . . How come I'm being followed, if
They don't know? First a guy with a beard, then a kid in
a red snow suit. *I* seen them together. Listen, you frigg-
ing little jocko, you better *think*, I'm telling you—you better think hard!" He poked again with his stiff and dirty
finger. And again. "I always knew, see, I always *knew*
that there was a million bucks waiting for me somewhere,
if I only kept my eyes open. What the Hell is a guy
like me doing unloading crates in the fruit market, when
I got plans for a million? And then—" His voice sank
and his eyes narrowed. "—this Professor Whitman come
along and put up at the Eagle Hotel. I caught his act in
the sticks once, I been around. *First* I thought he was
practicing ventriloquism, *then* I found out about *you—
you* was the other voice in his room! And that's when I—"

Abruptly he stopped. The outside door opened with a
rusty squeal and footfalls sounded in the hall. Someone
knocked. Someone tried the knob. Someone said, "Sacheverell? Sacheverell?" and George clamped his hairy,
filthy hand over the captive's mouth. Sacheverell jerked
and twitched and rolled his eyes. The voice made a disappointed noise, the footfalls moved uncertainly, started

to retreat. And then Sacheverell kicked out at George's crotch. The man grunted, cursed, lost his grip—

"*Help!*" Sacheverell cried. "*Help! Help! Save me!*"

Fists beat on the door, the glass in the back window crashed and fell to the floor, a weasened old-man's face peered through the opening, withdrew. George ran to the door, then turned to chase Sacheverell, who fled, shrieking hysterically. A tiny figure in a red snow-suit squeezed through the bars of the back window and ran to pull the bolt on the door. Someone in boots and a plaid jacket and a woolen watch-cap burst in, melting snow glittering on a big black beard.

"Save me!" Sacheverell screamed, dashing from side to side. "He attacked Professor Whitman and knocked him down *and he didn't get up again—*"

George stooped, picking up the chair, but the red snow-suit got between his legs and he stumbled. The chair was jerked from his hands, he came up with his fists clenched and the bearded person struck down with the chair. It caught him across the bridge of the nose with a crunching noise, he fell, turned over, stayed down. Silence.

Sacheverell hiccupped. Then he said, "Why are you wearing *men's* clothing, Princess Zaga?"

"A bearded man attracts quite enough attention, thank you," the Princess said, disengaging the chain. "No need to advertise . . . Let's get out of here." She picked him up and the three of them went out into the black, deserted street, boarded-shut windows staring blindly. The snow fell thickly, drifting into the ravaged hall and into the room where George's blood, in a small pool, had already begun to freeze.

"There's our car, Sacheverell," said the man in the red snow-suit, thrusting a cigar into his child-size, jaded old face. "What a time—"

"I assume you are still with the carnival, General Pinkey?"

"No, kiddy. The new owners wouldn't recognize the union, so we quit and retired on Social Security in Sarasota. You'll like it there. Not that the unions are much better, mind you: Bismarkian devices to dissuade the working classes from industrial government on a truly Marxian, Socialist-Labor basis. We got a television set, kiddy."

"And look who's waiting for you—" Princess Zaga opened the station wagon and handed Sacheverell inside. There, in the back seat, was the hugest, the vastest, the fattest woman in the world.

"Princess Opal!" Sacheverell cried, leaping into her arms—and was buried in the wide expanse of her bosom and bathed in her warm Gothick tears. She called him her Precious and her Little Boy and her very own Peter Pan.

"It was Madame Opal who planned this all," Princess Zaga remarked, starting the car and driving off. General Pinkey lit his cigar and opened a copy of *The Weekly People.*

"Yes, I did, yes, I did," Mme. Opal murmured, kissing and hugging Sacheverell. "Oh, how neglected you are! Oh, how thin! We'll have a tea-party, just like we used to, the very best doll dishes; we'll see you eat nice and we'll wash you and comb you and put ribbons around your neck."

Sacheverell began to weep. "Oh, it was *awful* with George," he said.

"Never mind, never mind, he didn't know any better," Mme. Opal said, soothingly.

"The Hell he didn't!" snapped Princess Zaga.

"Predatory capitalism," General Pinkey began.

"Never mind, never mind, forget about it, darling, it was only a bad dream . . ."

Sacheverell dried his tears on Mme. Opal's enormous spangled-velvet bosom. "George was very *mean* to me," he said. "He treated me *very* mean. But worst of all, you know, Madame Opal, he *lied* to me—he lied to me all the time, and I almost believed him—that was the most horrible part of all: I almost believed that I was a monkey."

Take Wooden Indians

Down from the streets (morning air already gray and bitter with motor exhaust and industrial fumes), into the jampacked subway he passed. His clothes, though mildly incongruous in that unhappy throng, brought him no special measure of attention. Weary, wary, cynical, grim, displeasured indifference lying on each countenance like an oily film, the folk stared not so much at him as over and through him.

He fought to keep his feet, struggled to maintain his balance. This, merely the antechamber to everyday existence, was difficult enough. Add to it the need to be constantly on the lookout for the Wooden Indian Society and he felt he had reason to be tense and jumpy. "Benedict, a leading modern free-form sculptor in wood—" Ha!

Twice he had been aware that they had tailed him as far as Times Square. Twice he had lost them. A third time—

The man in the faintly funny-looking clothes (his name was Don Benedict, but some called him "Dusty") paused for a minute under one of the red-lettered wooden signs, took a quick look at the paper in his hand (more, it almost seemed, to reassure himself that it was still there than to scan the contents), did an about-face and started back the way he had come. By and by he came to a stairway which he ascended for five steps, then turned around and went down. At the bottom—

At the bottom of it all was Elwell, and Elwell was dead: not from the cough which had been tearing him apart for years, but dead of a slippery little patch of ice no bigger than a man's hand. Elwell, dying, with blood in the corners of his mouth, holding Don's hand in a grip which the younger man could feel the heat going out of.

"But it belongs to the WIS," Don had protested.

And Elwell: "No, Don, no—it belongs to me. I formed it. I proved it."

"They'll never allow—"

With a desperate, slow intensity, shaking his head, Elwell had explained. Reluctantly, Don agreed. It seemed to him that he was agreeing to no more than the first risk. But then, with Elwell dead, and the WIS turning against them both—first with coldness, then with clamor, then with a silent tenacity more disturbing than either —Don Benedict came to see that it was not only the beginning which was his, but that it was all his. Forevermore.

At the bottom of the stairs, he saw the man out of the corner of his eye, eye intent upon feet, feet pacing out the pattern. He stopped for a moment, intending only to turn. And stayed stopped. The man (it was Anders) took hold of his arm as if to urge him on.

"I'm coming with you, Benedict." Eyes burning, voice iron-hard.

"I'm going alone."

"You've betrayed the trust, used what belongs to all of us, used it for yourself alone. The WIS—"

As always, so now, the Wooden Indian Society undoing themselves: Anders, trembling with fury, unawarely released his grip. Don placed the cushion of his palm under Ander's chin, thrust forward and upward with all his strength. And at once, swift—but not forgetting himself, not breaking into a run—he finished what he had to do. Anders staggered back, arms flailing, feet failing at purchase; then Don, turning his head at the last, saw him fall, the electric lights glaring on the white-tiled walls.

His foot jarred, as always, missing the familiar flooring by an inch. He adjusted his gait to the flagstone pave of the alley. It stretched before him and behind him for twenty feet in either direction. There was no one in sight.

About halfway along, there was a deep recess, a bricked-up door, and here Don hid until he was quite sure that Anders was not coming through. There was never any certainty that the WIS had not pieced it together, spying—somehow—pieced it together, bit by bit. There was always that tension, even here—though less, much less. After all, if they did get through, it would no longer be him that they were primarily after. It would be Demuth's. And Demuth's could look out for themselves.

Waiting, ears alert, he recalled the last meeting of the WIS he had dared attend. Mac Donald, eyes blazing deep in their sockets, had broken into Derwentwater's measured phrases, thrust a shaking finger into Don's face.

"Do you call yourself a Preservationist? Yes or no? Stand up and be counted!"

Staunchly, he had faced him, had answered. "I consider myself a philosophical Preservationist. I do not believe in violent—"

Face convulsed, fists clenched in the air, *"Traitor! Traitor!"* Mac Donald had screamed.

Not yielding, Don started to speak, got no further than Elwell's name, when Mac Donald—and Anders, Gumpert, De Giovanetti, almost all of them, in fact—had drowned him out with their outcry, their threats. *How much had Demuth's paid him? How much had he sold out for?*

Demuth's! Don mouthed the name scornfully. As if he would touch their tainted money. He had learned, the hard way, that Elwell was right all along, that the WIS were fanatics who would shrink from nothing. Well, he wasn't doing any shrinking, either.

Don Benedict came out of the niche—Anders wasn't going to get through this time, that was clear—and walked on down the alley. In less than a minute, he came out into a courtyard where heaps of chips and sawdust lay on one side and heaps of hay on the other. A man in dung-smeared boots came out of the building to the left with a bucket of milk in his hand. He paused, squinted, tugged his tobacco-stained beard and put down the bucket.

"Hey, Dusty! Glad to see you," he greeted the newcomer. "You just get into town?"

"Ee-yup," said Don/Dusty. "How you, Swan?"

Swan said he was fine, and inquired about things up in Sairacuse.

"Capital," said Dusty. "Hay's bringing a fine price—"

Swan groaned, spat into the sawdust. "Good for dem, maybe. Not for me. I tink you been at de bottle, hey, Dusty? You look yumpy, like always, ven you yust come in."

"Bottle? I get little enough out of any bottle I buy. My damned brother-in-law" (it was true—he had forgotten about Walter; it would be nice if he never had to remember) "drinks my liquor, smokes my cigars, wears my shirts, and spends my money."

Swan groaned sympathetically, picked up the bucket. "Vy don't you kick him de hell out?"

Nice advice, would be a pleasure to take it. Of course, Mary wouldn't be able to stand it. Poor rabbity Mary.

"All I need is to get back to work. That'll fix me up." Don/Dusty waved, continued on his way across the yard and went into the doorway of the tall brick building to the right. Inside, it was cool and dark and smelled of wood and paint.

Dusty took a deep breath and began to smile.

He started up the stairs, ignoring the painted hand with outstretched finger and word *Office* on the first floor. By the time he reached the second floor, his smile was very broad. Softly, he began to sing "Aura Lee" and went in through the open door.

The big loft was dark; little light came in through the small and dirty windows, but at regular intervals a gas-jet flared. Dusty paused to greet his friends. Silently they stared down at him, peering from underneath the hands shading their eyes, stretching out their arms in wordless welcome, plumage blazing in a frenzy of colors.

"Hello, there, Tecumseh! How, Princess Redwing! Osceola, Pocahontas—"

A red-faced little man in a long striped apron trotted out into view, two tufts of snowy hair decorating his cheeks, a hat of folded newsprint on his head.

"Dusty, Dusty, I'm darned glad to see you!" he exclaimed.

"Hello, Charley Voles. How's everything at C. P. Hennaberry's?"

Charley shook his head. "Good *and* bad," he said. "Good *and* bad. Oscar snagged his hand on a nail moving some plunder at home and it festered up something terrible. We was feared it was going to mortify at first, but I guess he's on the mend at last. Can't work, though, no-o-o-o, can't work. And Hennery was too numerous with the drink, fell off the wagon again and I think he must still be in the Bridewell, unless'n maybe his sentence is up today. Meanwhile, the work is piling high. Thunderation, yes—fly-figures, rosebuds, pompeys, *two* Turks under orders—"

"*Two?*" Dusty paused with his arms half out of his coat sleeves, whistled.

Charley nodded proudly. "Gent in Chicago opening up a big emporium, two Turks *and* two Sir Walters. Only thing is—" his ruddy little face clouded—"gent is clamcring for delivery, says if he don't get 'em soon he'll order from Detroit. And you know what *that* means, Dusty: Let trade get away and it never comes back. Why, the poor Major is pulling his whiskers out worrying. 'Course, with you back in town—"

Dusty, tying his apron, pursed his lips. "Well, now, Charley—now you know, I never did fancy my work much on the special figures. I want to help Major Hennaberry all I can, but—" He shook his head doubtfully and started to lay out his tools.

Charley Voles tut-tutted. "Oscar and Hennery was working on the Turks when they was took sick or drunk. *I* had the top three of a Sir Walter done, but I had to leave off to handle a couple of prior orders on sachems. Now if you'll take on the sachems, I can finish the specials. How's that strike you?"

Dusty said it struck him fine. He strode over to the hydraulic elevator shaft and gave two piercing whistles.

"Boy!" he shouted. "Boy! Benny?"

A treble from the office floor inquired if that was him, Mr. Dusty, and said it would be right up. A noise of gasping and stomping from below indicated that someone else would be right up, too.

"I want some breakfast, Benny," Dusty said, tossing him a coin. "Here's a quarter of a dollar. Get me the usual—eggs, pancakes, sausages, toast, coffee and crullers. Get some beer for Mr. Voles. And you can keep the change. *Hello*, Major Hennaberry!"

The elevator cage surged slowly into view. First came Major Hennaberry's bald spot, then his custard-colored eyes, magenta nose and cheeks, pepper-and-salt whiskers, and, gradually, the Major himself, breathing noisily. In his hand he held a booklet of some sort.

Slowly and sybillantly, the Major moved forward, shook Dusty's hand.

"Don't know what's come over the American mechanic nowadays," he said at last, asthmatically. "Can't seem to keep himself safe, sober, or in the city limits, and acts as if Hell has let out for noon. . . . Got some lovely white pine for you, my boy, fresh up from the spar yards. Don't waste a minute—soon's you get outside of your victuals, commence work. Draw on the cashier if you want anything in advance of wages: a dollar, two dollars, even a half-eagle.

"Never had so many orders nor so few men to execute them since starting in business," the Major wheezed on. "Even had Rat Nolan on picket duty for me, combing South Street and the Bowery—offered him three dollars apiece for any carvers he could find. Nothing, couldn't find a one. It's the catalog that's done the boom, my lad. The power of advertising. Here—read it whilst you eat; be pleased to have your opinion."

Hissing and panting, he made his way back to the elevator, jerked the rope twice, slowly sank from sight.

Dusty turned to the old artisan. "Charley," he said, slowly, as if he hadn't quite determined his words, "hear anything about Demuth's?"

Charley made a face. "What would you want to hear about that ugly, pushy outfit?"

Changing, somewhat, his point of inquiry, Dusty asked, "Well, now, have you ever thought about the significance of the wooden Indian in American history?"

The old man scratched the left fluff of whisker. "By crimus, that's a high-toned sentence," he said, rather dubiously. "Hmm. Well, all's I can tell you—history, hey?—the steam engine was the makings of the show-figure trade, tobacco shop or otherwise. Certainly. All of us old-timers got our start down on South Street, carving figureheads for sailing craft. That was about the time old Hennaberry got his major's commission in the Mercantile Zouaves—you know, guarding New York City from the Mexicans. Yes, sir. But when the steam come *in*, figureheads went *out*. Well, 'twasn't the end of the world."

And he described how he and his fellow-artists had put their talents at the disposal of the show-figure trade, up to then a rather haphazard commerce. "History, hey? Well, I have had the idea it's sort of odd that as the live Indian gets scarcer, the wooden ones gets numerouser. But how come you to ask, Dusty?"

Carefully choosing his words, Dusty asked Charley to imagine a time in the far-off future when wooden Indians—show figures of any sort—were no longer being carved.

Had, in fact, suffered for so long a universal neglect that they had become quite rare. That gradually in-

terest in the sachems revived, that men began to collect
them as if they had been ancient marble statues, began
to study all that could be learned about them.

That some of these collectors, calling themselves the
Wooden Indian Society, had been consumed with grief
at the thought of the debacle which overtook the figures
they had grown to love. Had claimed to see in the decline
and death of this native art a dividing line in American
history.

"It was like, Charley, it was like this was the end of
the old times altogether," Don went on, "the end of the
Good Old Days, the final defeat of native crafts and
native integrity by the new, evil forces of industrialism.
And they thought about this and it turned them bitter
and they began to brood. Until finally they began to plan
how they could undo what had been done. They believed that if they could travel from their time to—to our
time, like traveling from here to, say, Brooklyn—"

How much of this could Charley grasp? Perhaps better
not to have tried.

Don/Dusty spoke more rapidly. "That if they could
reach this time period, they could preserve the wooden
Indian from destruction. And then the great change for
the worse would never occur. The old days and the old
ways would remain unchanged, or at least change
slowly."

"You mean they got this idea that if they could
change what happened to the wooden Indians, they
could maybe change the course of American history?"

Dusty nodded.

Charley laughed. "Well, they were really crazy—I mean
they would be, if there was to be such people, wouldn't
they? Because there ain't no way—"

Dusty blinked. Then his face cleared. "No, of course there isn't. It was just a moody dark thought . . . Ah, here comes Ben with my breakfast."

Charley lifted his beer off the laden tray, gestured his thanks, drank, put down the glass with a loud "Hah" of satisfaction. Then a sudden thought creased his face. "Now leave me ask you this, Dusty. Just what could ever happen to destroy such a well-established and necessary business as the show-figure business? Hmm?"

Dusty said that these people from the Wooden Indian Society, in this sort of dark thought he'd had, had looked into matters real thoroughly. And they came to believe very deeply, very strongly, that the thing which killed the wooden Indian, and in so doing had changed American history so terribly for the worst, had been the invention and marketing of an Indian made of cast-iron or zinc. An Indian which would have no life, no soul, no heart, no grace—but which would never wear out or need to be replaced.

And so it would sell—sell well enough to destroy the carvers' craft—but would destroy the people's love for the newer show figures at the same time.

Charley looked shocked. "Why, that'd be a terrible thing, Dusty—a thing which it'd cut a man to the heart! Cast-iron! Zinc! But I tell you what—if there ever was to be an outfit which'd do a thing like that, there'd be only one outfit that would. Demuth's. That's who. Ain't I right?"

Dusty lowered his head. In a low, choked voice, he said, "You're right."

Dusty propped the catalog against a short piece of pine, read as he ate.

"I don't know what it is," he said to old Charley, "but I have such an appetite here. I never eat breakfast at all when I'm—" He stopped, put a piece of sausage in his mouth, intently began to read.

We would respectfully solicit from the Public generally an inspection of our Large and Varied Assortment of WOODEN SHOW FIGURES *which we are constantly manufacturing for all classes of business, such as* SEGAR STORES, WINES & LIQUORS, SHIP CHANDLERS, INSTRUMENT MAKERS, DRUGGISTS, YANKEE NOTIONS, UMBRELLA, CLOTHING, CHINA TEA STORES, GUNSMITHS, BUTCHERS, &C, &C. *Our Figures are both carved and painted in a manner which cannot be excelled, are durable and designed and executed in a highly artistic manner; and are furnished at noncompetitive low prices. We are constantly receiving orders for statues and emblematic signs, and can furnish same of any required design with promptness.*

The sausage was fresh and savory; so was the coffee. Dusty chewed and swallowed with relish, slowly turned the pages of the catalog.

OUR NUMBER 23. Fly-figure, male 5 ft. high, bundle of 20 in outstretched hand (r.), usual colors. A nice staple type Show Figure no moderate-sized bus. need feel ashamed to display. At rival establishments, UP TO $75. *C. P. Hennaberry's Price: $50 even (with war-bonnet, $55).*

Note: Absolutely impos. to cite trade-in values *via* mails, as this depends on age, size, condition of fig., also state of market @ time.

OUR NUMBER 24. Same as above, with musket instead of tomahawk.

> *OUR NUMBER 36. Turk, male 6 ft. high, for*
> *shops which sell the fragrant Ottoman weed, poly-*
> *chrome Turk holding long leaf betw. both hands,*
> *choice of any two colors on turban. A. C. P. HENNA-*
> *BERRY SPECIAL: $165. (with beard & long pipe,*
> *$5 extra).*

They went upstairs after Dusty had finished his break-fast, pausing on the third (or second-hand figures) floor, to greet Otto and Larry.

Young Larry was still considered a learner and was not yet allowed to go beyond replacing arms, hands, noses, and other extra parts.

Otto, to be sure, was a master carver, but Otto had several strikes against him. In his youth, in his native Tyrol, Otto had studied sacred iconography; in his maturity, in America, Otto had studied drinking. As a result, when he was mellow, unless he was carefully super-vised, his Indians had a certain saintly quality to them, which made purchasers feel somehow guilty. And when, on the other hand, Otto was sobering up, a definite measure of apocalyptic horror invariably appeared in his sachems which frightened buyers away.

As a result, Otto was kept at doing extras—bundles of cigars, boxes of cigars, bundles of tobacco leaf, coils of tobacco leaf, twists of the same, knives, tomahawks, all to be held in the figures' hands—and at equally safe tasks like stripping off old paint, sanding, repainting, fin-ishing.

He nodded sadly, eyes bloodshot, to Dusty and Char-ley, as he applied ochre and vermillion to a war bonnet. "Ho, Chesus," he groaned softly.

Up in the woodloft, they made an inspection of the spars. "Now you needn't pick the ones I started, of course," Charley said. "Take fresh ones, if you like. 'Course, all's I did was I drawn the outlines and just kind of chiseled 'em in. And put the holes in on top for the bolts."

Dusty stood back and squinted. "Oh, I guess they'll be all right, Charley," he said. "Well, let's get 'em downstairs."

This done, Charley went back to work on the Sir Walter, carefully chiseling *Virginia Tobacco* in bas-relief on the cloak.

Dusty took up his axe and blocked out approximate spaces for the head, the body down to the waist, roughly indicated the division of the legs and feet. Then he inserted the iron bolt into the five-inch hole prepared for it, and tilted back the spar so that the projecting part of the bolt rested on a support. When he had finished head and trunk, he would elevate the lower part of the figures in the same way.

Finally, finished with blocking out, he picked up mallet and chisel.

"I now strike a blow for liberty," he said.

Smiling happily, he began to chip away. The song he sang was "Aura Lee."

Don/Dusty Benedict let himself into his studio quietly —but not quietly enough. The sharp sound of a chair grating on the floor told him that his brother-in-law was upstairs. In another second, Walter told him so himself in an accent more richly Southern, probably, than when he had come North as a young boy.

"We're upstairs, Don."

"Thank you for the information," Don muttered.

"We're *upstairs*, Don."

"Yes, Walter. All right. I'm coming."

Walter welcomed him with a snort. "Why the hell do

you always wear those damn cotton-pickin' clothes when you go away? Not that it matters. I only wish *I* could just take up and go whenever the spirit moves me. Where was it you went this time?"

"Syracuse," Don mumbled.

"Syracuse. America's new vacation land." Walter laughed, not pleasantly. "Don, you really expect me to believe you? Syracuse! Why not just say to me, frankly, 'I've got a woman'? That's all. I wouldn't say another word." He poured himself several drams of Don's Scotch.

Not much you wouldn't, Don thought. Aloud, "How are you, Mary?" His sister said that she was just fine, sighed, broke off the sigh almost at once, at her husband's sour look.

Walter said, "Roger Towns was up. Another sale for you, another commission for me. Believe me, I earned it—gave him a big talk on how the Museum of Modern Art was after your latest. So he asked me to use my influence. He'll be back—he'll take it. This rate, the Modern Art *will* be after you before long."

Don privately thought this unlikely, though anything was possible in this world of no values. He wasn't a "modern, free-form" artist, or, for that matter, any kind of artist at all. He was a craftsman—in a world which had no need for craftsmen.

"But *only*—" another one of the many qualities which made Walter highly easy to get along without: Walter was a finger-jabber—"but *only* if you finish the damned thing. About time, isn't it? I mean vacations are fine, but the bills . . ."

Don said, "Well, my affairs are in good hands—namely, yours."

Walter reared back. "If that's meant as a dig—! Listen, I can get something else to do any time I want. In fact, I'm looking into something else *now* that's damned promising. Firm sells Canadian stocks. Went down to see them yesterday. 'You're just the kind of man we're interested in, Mr. Swift,' they told me. 'With your vast experience and your knowledge of human nature. . . .'"

Walt scanned his brother-in-law's face, defying him to show signs of the complete disbelief he must have known Don felt. Don had long since stopped pretending to respond to these lies. He only ignored them—only put up with Walt at all—for his sister's sake. It was for her and the kids only that he ever came back.

"I'd like a drink," Don said, when Walt paused.

Dinner was as dinner always was. Walt talked almost constantly, mostly about Walt. Don found his mind wandering again to the Wooden Indian Society. Derwentwater, ending every speech with *"Delendo est Demuth's!"* Gumpert and his eternal "Just one stick of dynamite, Don, just one!" De Giovanetti growling, "Give us the Equation and we'll do it ourselves!"

Fools! They'd have to learn every name of those who had the hideous metal Indian in mind, conduct a massacre in Canal Street. Impossible. Absurd.

No, Elwell had been right. Not knowing just how the Preservationist work was to be done, he had nonetheless toiled for years to perfect a means to do it. Only when his work was done did he learn the full measure of WIS intransigence. And, after learning, had turned to Don.

"Take up the torch," he pleaded. "Make each sachem such a labor of love that posterity cannot help but preserve it."

And Don had tried. The craft had been in him and struggling to get out all the time, and he'd never realized it!

Slowly the sound of Walter's voice grew more impossible to ignore.

". . . and you'll need a new car, too. I can't drive that heap much longer. It's two years *old*, damn it!"

"I'd like a drink," Don said.

By the time Edgar Feld arrived, unexpectedly, Don had had quite a few drinks.

"I took the liberty not only of calling unheralded, but of bringing a friend, Mr. White," the art dealer said. He was a well-kept little man. Mr. White was thin and mild.

"Any friend of Edgar's is someone to be wary of," Don said. "Getchu a drink?"

Walt said he was sure they'd like to see the studio. There was plenty of time for drinks.

"Time?" Don muttered. "Whaddayu know about time?"

"Just step this way," Walt said loudly, giving his brother-in-law a deadly look. "We think, we rather think," he said, taking the wraps off the huge piece, "of calling this the Gemini—"

Don said genially that they had to call it *something* and that Gemini (he supposed) sounded better than Diseased Kidney.

Mr. White laughed.

Edgar Feld echoed the laugh, though not very heartily. "Mr. Benedict has the most modest, most deprecatory attitude toward his work of any modern artist—working in wood or in any other medium."

Mr. White said that was very commendable. He asked Don if he'd like a cigar.

"I would, indeed!" the modest artist assented. "Between cigarette smoke, gasoline and diesel fumes, the air is getting unfit to breathe nowadays. . . . So Edgar is conning you into modern art, hey, Whitey?"

"Ho, ho!" Edgar Feld chuckled hollowly.

"Nothing better than a good cigar." Don puffed his contentment.

White said, with diffidence, that he was only just beginning to learn about modern art. "I used to collect Americana," he explained.

Edgar Feld declared that Mr. White had formerly had a collection of wooden Indians. His tone indicated that, while this was not to be taken seriously, open mockery was uncalled for.

Don set down the glass he had brought along with him. No, White was hardly WIS material. He was safe. "Did you really? Any of Tom Millards, by any chance? Tom carved some of the sweetest fly-figures ever made."

Mr. White's face lit up. "Are you a wooden Indian buff, too?" he cried. "Why, yes, as a matter of fact, I had two of Millard's fly-figures, and one of his pompeys—"

Walt guffawed. "What are fly-figures and pompeys?"

"A fly-figure is a sachem with an outstretched arm," Don said. "A pompey is a black boy."

"A rosebud," Mr. White happily took up the theme, "is a squaw figure. A scout is one who's shading his eyes with one hand. Tom Millard, oh, yes! And I had some by John Cromwell, Nick Collins, Thomas V. Brooks, and Tom White—my namesake. Listen! Maybe you can tell me. Was Leopold Schwager a manufacturer or an artist?"

Don Benedict laughed scornfully. "Leopold Schwager was a junk-dealer! Bought old figures for five, ten dollars, puttied and painted 'em, sold 'em for twenty-five. Cobb!" he exclaimed suddenly. "You have any Cobbs, Mr. White?"

"Cobb of Canal Street? No, I always wanted one, but—"

Edgar Feld looked at Walter Swift, cleared his throat. "Now, Don—"

"Cobb of Canal Street," Don said loudly, "never used a mallet. No, sir. Drove the chisel with the palm of his hand. And then there was Charley Voles—"

Feld raised his voice above Don's. "Yes, we must talk about his fascinating though obsolete art sometime. Don't you want to step a little closer to the Gemini, Mr. White?"

"Yes, White, damn it, buy the damned Gemini so they'll quit bothering us and we can get back to *real* art," said Don.

And forget about Walter, Demuth's and the WIS, he said to himself.

Next morning, he tried to remember what had happened after that. White *had* taken the shapeless mass of wood Walt called Gemini. (What would he tell Roger Down, the private collector? Some good, whopping lie, depend on it.) He was sure he remembered White with his checkbook out. And then? A confused picture of White examining the polished surface, pointing at something—

Don Benedict badly wanted a cup of coffee. His room was just off the studio, and once there had been a hot-plate there, but Walt had ordered it removed on the grounds of danger. So now Don had to go up to Walt's apartment when he wanted a cup of coffee. That was how Walt liked everything to be: little brother coming to big brother. Well, there was no help for it. Don went upstairs, anticipating cold looks, curt remarks, at every step.

However, Walt was sweetness itself this morning. The coffee was ready; Walt had poured it even before Don entered the kitchen. After he finished his cup (made from unboiled water, powdered coffee, ice-cold milk)

Walt urged another on him. Rather than speak, he took it.

Don knew, by the falsely jovial note of Walter's voice, that Something Was Up. He gulped the tepid slop and rose. "Thanks. See you later, Walter—"

But Walter reached out his hand and took him by the arm. "Let's talk about the Lost Dutchman Mine. ("The *what?*") The Spanish Treasure. ("I don't—") Spelled E-l-w-e-l-l," said Walter, with an air at once sly and triumphant.

Don sat down heavily.

"Don't know what I mean by those figures of speech? Odd. You did last night. Matter of fact, they were yours," said Walter, mouth pursed with mean amusement. He would refresh Don's memory. Last night, Mr. White had asked Don how he had come to have so much contemporary knowledge about the making of wooden Indians. Don had laughed. "An old prospector I befriended left me the map to the Lost Dutchman Mine," he had said, waving his glass. "To the Spanish Treasure."

When Mr. White, puzzled, asked what he meant, Don had said, "It's easy. You just walk around the horses." Now what, just exactly, had Don meant by that?

"I must have been drunk, Walter."

"Oh, yes, you were drunk, all right. But *in vino veritas* . . . Now I've been thinking it out very carefully, Don. It seems to me that 'the old desert rat' you spoke of must have been that fellow Elwell, who slipped on the ice two winters ago. The one you got to the hospital and visited regularly till he died. Am I right, Don? Am I?"

Don nodded miserably. "Damn liquor," he added.

"*Now* we're making progress," said Walt. "*Okay*. Now about this map to the mine. I know he left you that damn

notebook. I know that. But I looked it over very carefully
and it was just a lot of figures scribbled—equations, or
what ever th' hell you call 'em. But it had something else
in it, didn't it? Something you took out. We'll get to just
what by and by. So—and it was right after that that you
started going on these vacations of yours. Made me
curious. Those funny clothes you wore."

Stiff and tight, Don sat in the bright, neat kitchen and
watched the waters rise. There was nothing for him here
and now, except for Mary and the children, and his love
for them had been no more selfish than theirs for him.
He had been glad when Walt first appeared, happy when
they married, unhappy when Walt's real nature appeared,
very pleased when the chance occurred to offer "a position" to his brother-in-law. The misgivings felt when a few
people actually offered to buy the shapeless wooden
things he had created almost aimlessly (he knowing that
he was not a sculptor but a craftsman) vanished when he
saw it was the perfect setup for keeping Mary and the
kids supported.

Of course, after a while Don had been able to arrange
the majority of the "sales." The waste of time involved
in hacking out the wooden horrors which "private collectors" bought was deplorable. The whole system was
dreadfully clumsy, but its sole purpose—to create a world
in which Walter would be satisfied and Mary happy—
was being fulfilled, at any rate.

Or had been.

What would happen now, with Walter on the verge of
finding out everything?

"And Syracuse—what a cottonpickin' alibi! I figured
you had a woman hid away for sure, wasting your time
when you should have been working, so—well, I wanted
to find out who she was, where she lived. That's why I

always went through your pockets when you came back
from these 'vacations'—"

"Walter, you didn't!"

But of course he knew damned well that Walter did.
Had known for some time that Walter was doing it. Had
acted accordingly. Instead of hiding the evidence, he had
deliberately planted it, and in such a way that it couldn't
possibly fail to add up to exactly one conclusion.

"What a lot of junk!" Walter jeered. "Like somebody
swept the floor of an antique shop and dumped it all
in your pocket. Ticket stubs with funny old printing,
clippings from newspapers of years back—and all like
that. *However—*" he jabbed a thick, triumphant finger at
Don—"money is money, no matter how old it is. Right?
Damned right! Old dollar bills, old gold pieces. Time after
time. You weren't very cautious, old buddy. So now—
just what *is* this 'Spanish Treasure' that you've been tapping? Let's have the details, son, or else I'll be mighty
unhappy. And when I'm unhappy, Mary is too . . ."

That was very true, Don had realized for some time
now. And if Mary couldn't protect herself, how could
the youngsters escape?

"I'm tired of scraping along on ten per cent, you see,
Don. I got that great old American ambition: I want to
be in business for myself. And you are going to provide
the capital. So—again, and for the last time—let's have
the details."

Was this the time to tell him? And, hard upon the
thought, the answer came: Yes, the time was now, time
to tell the truth. At once his heart felt light, joyous; the
heavy weight (long so terribly, constantly familiar) was
removed from him.

"Mr. Elwell—the old gentleman who slipped on the
ice; you were right about that, Walter—" Walter's face

slipped into its familiar, smug smile. "Mr. Elwell was a
math teacher at the high school down the block. Imagine
it—a genius like him, pounding algebra into the heads of
sullen children! But he didn't let it get him down, because that was just his living. What he mainly lived for
were his space-time theorems. 'Elwell's Equations,' we
called them—"

Walter snorted. "Don't tell me the old gimp was a time
traveler and left you his time machine?"

"It wasn't a machine. It was only a—well, I guess it
was a sort of map, after all. He tried to explain his
theories to me, but I just couldn't understand them. It
was kind of like chess problems—I never could understand *them*, either. So when we arranged that I was going
to visit 1880, he wrote it all down for me. It's like a pattern. You go back and forth and up and down and after
a while—"

"After a while you're in 1880?"

"That's right."

Walter's face had settled in odd lines. "I thought you
were going to try not telling me what I'd figured out for
myself," he said in the cutting exaggeration of his nor-
mally exaggerated Southern drawl. This was the first
time he had used it on Don, though Don had heard it
used often enough on Mary and the kids. "The map, and
all those clues you were stupid enough to leave in your
pockets, and the stupidest of all—carving your own
squiggle signature into all those dozens of old wooden
Indians. Think I can't add?"

"But that was Canal Street, 1880, and this is now," said
Don in a carefully dismal-sounding voice. "I thought it
was safe."

Walter looked at him. Walter—who had never earned
an ethical dollar in his life, and had scarcely bothered

to make a pretense of supporting his wife since Don's work had started to sell—asked, "All right, why 1880— and why wooden Indians?"

Don explained to him how he felt at ease there, how the air was fresher, the food tastier, how the Russians were a menace only to other Russians, how—and the sachems! What real, sincere pleasure and pride he got out of carving them.

They were *used!* Not like the silly modern stuff he turned out now, stuff whose value rested only on the fact that self-seekers like Edgar Feld were able to con critics and public into believing it was valuable.

Walt scarcely heard him. "But how much money can you make carving wooden Indians?"

"Not very much in modern terms. But you see, Walt— I invest."

And that was the bait in the trap he'd set and Walt rose to it and struck. "The market! Damn it to hell, of *course!*" The prospect of the (for once in his whole shoddy career) Absolutely Sure Thing, the Plunge which was certain to be a Killing, of moving where he could know without doubt what the next move would be, almost deprived Walter of breath.

"A tycoon," he gasped. "You could have been a tycoon and all you could think of was—"

Don said that he didn't want to be a tycoon. He just wanted to carve wooden—

"Why, I could make us better than tycoons! Kings! Emperors! One airplane—" He subsided after Don convinced him that Elwell's Equation could transport only the individual and what he had on or was carrying. "Lugers," he muttered. "Tommy-guns. If I'm a millionaire, I'll need bodyguards. Gould, Fisk, Morgan—they better watch out, that's all."

He slowly refocused on Don. "And *I'll* carry the map," he said.

He held out his hand. Slowly, as if with infinite misgivings, Don handed over to him the paper with Elwell's 1880 Equation.

Walter looked at it, lips moving, brows twisting, and Don recalled his own mystification when the old man had showed it to him.

"... *where* x *is one pace and* Y *is five-sixth of the hypotenuse of a right-angled triangle of which both arms are* x *in length* ..."

"Well," said Walter, "now let's get down to business." He rose, went off toward the living room, returned in a minute. Following him was a man with the tense, set face of a fanatic. He looked at Don with burning eyes.

"Anders!" cried Don.

"Where is the Equation?" Anders demanded.

"Oh, *I* got that," Walter said.

He took it out, showed a glimpse, thrust it in his pocket. He stepped back, put a chair between him and the WIS man.

"Not so fast," he said. "I got it and I'm keeping it. At least for now. So let's talk business. Where's the cash?"

As Anders, breathing heavily, brought out the roll of bills, "Oh, Walter, what have you done?" Don moaned. "Don't throw me in the bramble-bush, Brer Wolf!"

"Here is the first part of it," said Anders, ignoring his former WIS associate. "For this you agree to return to Canal Street, 1880, and destroy—by whatever means are available—the infamous firm of Demuth's. In the unlikely case of their continuing in the business after the destruction—"

"They won't. Best goon job money can buy; leave it to me."

Anders hesitated.

Walter promptly said, "No, you can't come along. Don't ask again. Just him and me. I'll need him for bird-dogging. I'll get in touch when we come back. As agreed, I bring back copies of the New York papers showing that Demuth's was blown up or burned down. On your way."

With one single hate-filled glance, not unmixed with triumph, at Don, Anders withdrew. The door closed. Walter laughed.

"You aren't—" Don began.

"Not a chance. Think I'm crazy? Let him and his crackpot buddies whistle for their money. No doubt you are wondering how I put two and two in a vertical column and added, hey, Donny boy? Well, once I figured out that the 'Prospector' was Elwell, and saw the WIS membership card in your pocket, I remembered that he and you used to go to those WIS meetings together, and I got in touch with them. They practically told me the whole story, but I wanted confirmation from you. All right, on your feet. We've got a pea patch to tear up."

While Walt was shaving, Don and Mary had a few minutes together.

"Why don't you just go, Don?" she begged. "I mean for good—away where he can't find you—and stay there. Never mind about me or the children. We'll make out."

"But wouldn't he take it out on you and them?"

"I said don't worry about us and I mean it. He's not all bad, you know. Oh, he might be, for a while, but that's just because he never really adjusted to living up North. Maybe if we went back to his home town—he always talks about it—I mean he'd be different there—"

He listened unhappily to her losing her way between wanting him out of her misery and hoping that the unchangeable might change.

"Mary," he broke in, "you don't have to worry any more. I'm taking Walt along and setting him up—really setting him up. And listen—" he wrote a name and address on the back of her shopping list—"go see this man. I've been investing money with his firm and there's plenty to take care of you and the kids—even if things go wrong with Walt and me. This man will handle all your expenses."

She nodded, not speaking. They smiled, squeezed hands. There was no need for embrace or kiss-the-children.

Whistling "Dixie," Walter returned. "Let's go," he said.

"Good-by, Don," said Mary.

"Good-by, Mary," said Don.

That afternoon, Don Benedict and Walter Swift, after visits to a theatrical costumer and a numismatist, entered the Canal Street subway station. Those who have had commerce with that crossroads of lower Manhattan know how vast, how labyrinthine, it is. Only a few glances, less than idly curious, were given them as they paced through the late Mr. Elwell's mathematical map. No one was present when they passed beneath a red-lettered sign reading "Canarsie Line" and vanished away.

As soon as he felt the flagstones beneath his feet, Walter whirled around and looked back. Instead of the white-tiled corridor, he saw a wet stone wall. For a moment, he swore feebly. Then he laughed.

"A pocketful of long green and another of gold eagles!" he exclaimed. "What shall we try for first? Erie or New York Central Common? No—first I want to see this place where you work. Oh, yes, I *do*. Obstinacy will get you nowhere. Lead on."

Wishing eventually to introduce Walt into Hennaberry's, Don had first taken him out to Canal Street.

Leopold Schwager's second-hand establishment was opposite, the sidewalk lined with superannuated sachems. Other establishments of the show-figure trade were within stonethrow, their signs, flags and figures making a brave display. Horsecars, cabs, drays, private carriages went clattering by.

Walter watched the passing scene with relish, leering at the women in what he evidently thought was the best 1880 masher's manner. Then he wrinkled his nose.

"Damn it all," he said, "I hadn't realized that the Hayes Administration smelled so powerfully of the horse. But I suppose *you* like it? Yes," he sneered, "you would. Well, enjoy it while you can. As soon as I manage to dig up some old plans, I propose to patent the internal combustion engine."

Don felt his skin go cold.

"John D. Rockefeller ought to be very, ver-ry interested," Walt said exultantly. "Why, five years from now, you won't know it's the same street . . . What're you pointing at?"

Don gestured to a scout-figure in full plumage outside a store whose awning was painted with the words, "*August Schwartz Segar Mfger Also Snuff, Plug, Cut Plug and Twist.*"

"One of mine," he said, pride mixed with growing resolve.

Walter grunted. "You won't have any time for that sort of thing any more; I'll need you myself. Besides—yes, why not? Introduce cigarette machinery. Start a great big advertising campaign, put a weed in the mouth of every American over the age of sixteen."

A drunken sailor lurched down the street singing "Sweet Ida Jane from Portland, Maine." Automatically, Don stepped aside to let him pass.

"But if you do that," he said, no longer doubting that Walter would if he could, "then there won't be any more—nobody will need—I mean my work—"

Walter said irritably, "I told you, you won't have the time to be piddling around with a mallet and chisel. And now let's see your wooden-Injun mine."

Acting as if he felt that nothing mattered any more, Don turned and led the way toward the brick building where C. E. Hennaberry, Show Figures and Emblematic Signs, did business. Ben the boy paused in his never-ending work of dusting the stock models to give a word and a wave in greeting. He stared at Walt.

In the back was the office, old Van Wart the clerk-cashier and old Considine the clerk-bookkeeper, on their high stools, bending over their books as usual. On the wall was a dirty photograph in a black-draped frame, with the legend "Hon. Wm. Marcy Tweed, Grand Sachem of the Columbian Order of St. Tammany" and underneath the portrait was the Major himself.

"So this is the place!" Walter declared, exaggerated Southern accent rolling richly. Major Hennaberry's friend, Col. Cox, sitting on the edge of the desk cutting himself a slice of twist, jumped as if stung by a minié-ball. His rather greasy sealskin cap slid over one eye.

"Get all kinds of people in here, don't you, Cephas?" he growled. "All's I got to say is: I was at Fredericksburg, I was at Shilo, and all's I got to say is: the only good Rebel is a dead Rebel!"

The Major, as Don well knew, hated Rebels himself, with a fervor possible only to a Tammany Democrat whose profitable speculations in cotton futures had been interrupted for four long, lean years. Don also knew that the Major had a short way of dealing with partisans of the Lost Cause, or with anyone else who had cost or threatened to cost him money—if he could just be brought to the point.

The Major looked up now, his eye lighting coldly on Walter, who gazed around the not overly clean room with a curious stare. "Yes, sir, might I serve you, sir? Nice fly-figure, maybe? Can supply you with a Highlander holding simulated snuff-mill at a tear-down price; no extra charge for tam-o-shanter. Oh, Dusty. Glad to see you—"

"Dusty" mumbled an introduction. How quickly things had changed—though not in any way for the better—and how paradoxically: because he had refused the WIS demand to change the past by violence so that modernism would be held off indefinitely, he was now condemned to see modernism arrive almost at once. Unless, of course . . .

"Brother-in-law, eh?" said Major Hennaberry, beginning to wheeze. "Dusty's done some speaking about you. Mmph." He turned abruptly to Don/Dusty. "What's all this, my boy, that Charley Voles was telling me—Demuth's coming up with some devilish scheme to introduce cast-iron show figures?" Dusty started, a movement noted by the keen though bloodshot eyes of his sometime employer. "Then it *is* true? Terrible thing, unconscionable. Gave me the liver complaint afresh, directly I heard of it. Been on medicated wine ever since."

Walt turned angrily on his brother-in-law. "Who told you to open your damn cotton-pickin mouth?"

The Major's purplish lips parted, moved in something doubtless intended for a smile.

"Now, gents," he said, "let's not quarrel. What must be must be, eh?"

"*Now* you're talking," said Walt, and evidently not realizing that he and Hennaberry had quite separate things in mind, he added: "Things will be different, but you'll get used to them."

Watching the Major start to wheeze in an unreasoning attack of rage, Dusty knew catalytic action was needed. "How about a drink, Major?" he suggested. "A Rat Nolan special?"

Unpurpling quickly, now merely nodding and hissing, the Major called for Ben. He took a coin out of his change purse and said: "Run over to Cooney's barrel-house and bring back some glasses and a pitcher of rum cocktail. And ask Cooney does he know where Nolan is. I got some business with him."

The boy left on the lope, and there was a short, tight silence. Then Col. Cox spoke, an anticipatory trickle already turning the corners of his mouth a wet brown. "I was at Island Number Ten, and I was at Kenisaw Mountain, and what I say is: the only good Rebel is a dead Rebel."

Walt grinned and said nothing until Ben came back with the drinks.

"Well, Scotch on the rocks it isn't," he said then, taking a brief sip, "but it's not bad."

He gave a brief indifferent glance at the shifty little man with Burnside whiskers who had come back with Ben, carrying the glasses.

"To science and invention!" cried Walt. "To progress!" He drained half his glass. His face turned green, then white. He started to slide sidewise and was caught by the little man in Burnsides.

"Easy does it, cully," said Mr. Rat Nolan, for it was he. "Dear, dear! I hope it's not a touch of this cholera morbus what's been so prevalent. Expect we'd better get him to a doctor, don't you, gents?"

Major Hennaberry said that there was not a doubt

about it. He walked painfully over to the elevator shaft, whistled shrilly. "Charley?" he called. "Larry? Oscar? Otto? Hennery? Get down here directly!"

Dusty emerged from his surprise at how neatly it had happened. He reached into Walter's coat pocket and took out the paper with Elwell's Equation on it. Now he was safe, and so was Canal Street, 1880. As for what would happen when Walter recovered from his strange attack—well, they would see.

The staff came out of the elevator cage with interest written large and plain upon their faces. Ben had evidently found time from his errand to drop a few words. Major Hennaberry gestured toward Walter, reclining, gray-faced, against the solicitous Mr. Rat Nolan, who held him in a firm grip.

"Gent is took bad," the Major explained. "Couple of you go out and see if you can find a cab—Snow Ferguson or Blinky Poole or one of those shunsoaps—and tell them to drive up by the alley. No sense in lugging this poor gent out the front."

Franz, Larry and Charley nodded and went out.

Otto stared. "No more vooden Indians, if he gets his vay," he said dismally at last. "Ho, Chesus," he moaned.

Dusty began, "Major, this is all so—"

"Now don't be woritting about your brother-in-law," said Rat Nolan soothingly. "For Dr. Coyle is a sovereign hand at curing what ails all pasty-faced, consumptive types like this one."

Dusty said that he was sure of it. "Where is Dr. Coyle's office these days?" he asked.

Mr. Rat Nolan coughed lightly, gazed at a cobweb in a corner of the ceiling. "The southwest passage to Amoy by way of the Straights is what the Doc is recommending for his patients—and he insists on accompanying them to see they follows doctor's orders, such being the degree of his merciful and tender-loving care . . ."

Dusty nodded approvingly.

"Ah, he's a rare one," said R. Nolan with enthusiasm, "is Bully Coyle, master of the *Beriah Jaspers* of the Black Star Line! A rare one and a rum one, and the Shanghaiing would be a half-dead trade without 'm, for it does use up men. And they leave on the morning tide."

There was a noise of *clomp-clomp* and metal harness-pieces jingled in the alley. Charley, Larry and Hennery came in, followed by a furtive-looking cabman with a great red hooked nose—Snow Ferguson, presumably, or Blinky Poole, or one of those shunsoaps.

"Ah, commerce, commerce," Rat Nolan sighed. "It waits upon no man's pleasure." He went through unconscious Walter's pockets with dispatch and divided the money into equal piles. From his own, he took a half-eagle which had been slightly scalloped and handed it to Dusty. "Share and share alike, and here's the regular fee. That's the spirit what made America great. Leave all them foreign monarchs beware . . . Give us a lift with the gent here, cullies . . ."

Charley took the head, Hennery and Otto the arms, while Larry and Ben held the feet. Holding the door open, the cabman observed, "Damfino-looking shoes this coffee-cooler's got on."

"Them's mine," said Rat Nolan instantly. "He'll climb the rigging better without 'em. Mind the door, cullies—don't damage the merchandise!"

Down the dim aisles the procession went, past the fly-figures, scout-figures, rosebuds, pompeys, Highlandmen, and Turks. The gas-jets flared, the shadows danced, the sachems scowled.

"If he comes to and shows fight," Major Hennaberry

called, "give him a tap with the mallet, one of you!"
He turned to Dusty, put a hand on his shoulder. "While
I realize, my boy, that no man can be called to account for the actions of his brother-in-law in this Great
Republic of ours, still I expect this will prove a lesson to
you. From your silence, I preceive that you agree. Your
sister now—hate to see a lady's tears—"

Dusty took a deep breath. The air smelled deliciously
of fresh wood and paint. "She'll adjust," he said. Mary
would be quite well off with the money from his invest-
ments. So there was no need, none at all, for his return.
And if the WIS tried to follow him, to make more trouble,
why—there was always Rat Nolan.

"Major Hennaberry, sir," he said vigorously, "we'll
beat Demuth's yet. You remember what you said when
the catalog came out, about the power of advertising?
We'll run their metal monsters into the ground and put a
wooden fly-figure on every street block in America!"

And they did.

The Vat

Dr. Lloyd was, you would think, successful enough to be satisfied, but that would be ignoring the fact that he was a reasonably normal man, with, perhaps, a little more drive than most.

Dr. Lloyd paused in the entrance to the hat store and lit a cigar. It was a very costly cigar, it was his last, his fingers trembled very lightly. *Damn* Peter Conrad! True, he had brought his troubles on his own head, but this didn't do Dr. Lloyd any good. Maybe this time—

He went inside.

A gray-haired and heavy-set man with a drooping mustache looked up and said, 'Good morning. I'll be with you shortly. . . . How do you like this one?' he asked the customer looking in the triple-mirror. This was a teen-age boy with acne and a long, thin neck, for whom nothing whatsoever was being done by a low-crowned hat with an all but imperceptible brim.

'Oh,' said the boy, swallowing. 'All right, I guess. Ah, how much money is it?' In another moment he was gone.

The hatter said, 'In my opinion the first five years of

adolescence should be passed in semi-monastic seclusion. The Government ought to set up refuges on remote islands, like bird sanctuaries. Eh?' Dr. Lloyd chuckled, thinly. 'If you're looking for something resembling what you've got on, I don't carry imported lines.'

'Perhaps not in hats. But in knowledge—?' Paused, smiled.

The proprietor, whose name was Alexis Franck, seemed puzzled. 'All right . . . I don't see what you're getting after, but if it's encyclopedias—'

Lloyd shook his head, blew out expensive smoke. 'It isn't. What do you know about *The Fair White Maiden Wedded To The Ruddy Man?*' And he raised his eyebrows.

Franck's face went grim. 'So you're—' He checked himself. The right-hand corner of his mouth twisted a bit. 'I know enough.'

'I'm sure you do. "So I'm—"?' He waited, but Franck said no more. 'Ever hear of a man called Peter Conrad?' Lloyd went on. 'No? Sure not? Well, how about books—say, *The Golden Tripod,* or one called *The Twelve Keys?*' Franck's upper lip curved just a trifle, and Lloyd took a breath. 'Or one called *Turba Philosophorum?*' Something flickered in Franck's eye, but he said nothing. Lloyd continued, 'I've been making some discreet inquiries—'

'You've been snooping, you mean!' the hatter said, scornful. 'I've had your kind around before— Oh, yes! Pickers of other men's brains, thieves of knowledge. Jackals, vultures. Well, you go on about your business, it seems to pay you well enough, by the look of your clothes and the smell of your cigar; go on away from here and leave me alone!'

He kept his voice low, but his anger was obvious.

Lloyd felt the tremble begin again in his fingers, laid his hands, palms flat, on the counter. 'Listen,' Lloyd said, 'I've gone as far as I can go by myself. We've got to work together . . .'

Something occurred suddenly to Alexis Franck, and it seemed to disturb him. 'What was that man's name? Peter Conrad? *Yes!*'

His visitor leaned heavily on the counter.

'Conrad,' he said. 'Conrad had a small factory down near the freight-yards, where he made bronze-castings. A pretense, a cover-up, like your hat shop. But I tell you that I am convinced that he was capable of making gold —pure gold, the kind that they say "smears like butter," it's so pure. . . .' His voice clicked in his throat.

'Then go back to him.'

Lloyd threw back his head and made a gesture of despair. 'I *can't!*' he exclaimed. 'He's dead . . . there was a fire, an explosion; they found him in the ruins. He was a fool! I—'

After a moment, Franck said, 'Bishop mentioned his name once, I think. You knew Bishop.'

Lloyd denied it. 'But his name keeps cropping up—'

'It would,' Alexis Franck muttered, 'Snooper. Jackal, vulture.'

'—although he seems to have dropped out of sight. Do you—'

'Haven't seen him in years. Rogue.'

'Oh, yes. I tell you, I've checked the stocks of various people who've had alchemical books . . . one dealer told me that in a trunkful from a cheap hotel, auction of un-claimed baggage, he found not only items stolen from every library around here, but a notebook in Bishop's own handwriting.'

Again the spark in Franck's eye. 'Haven't seen him in years,' he repeated. 'What kind of a notebook?'

'Records of alchemical and . . . other experiments. Not a very nice fellow. *But you collaborated with him!*'

Franck moved his lips in a snarl which framed his strong, yellow teeth. He didn't need any preaching of morality, he assured his visitor. 'I wanted knowledge. Had I wanted ethics—'

Lloyd said that *he* wanted knowledge, too. 'Tell you, they made *gold!*' he cried, striking the counter with his fist. He had been leaning over, now he straightened up. He no longer seemed debonair, his face was hot, and little white patches showed on his lip. 'Will you work with me?' he demanded. 'Or do I make discreet phone calls exposing your indiscreet—'

'Vulture. Jackal.'

'You mean, "Yes"?'

Franck grimaced, shrugged his lack of choice. He moved to lock the shop door, gestured the way into the back. Lloyd followed him through a wilderness of hatboxes, down a flight of steps, into a white-washed cellar. 'By the way,' Franck broke silence, 'have you any other partners?'

Lloyd smiled slowly, recognizing familiar equipment: alembic, pelican, athenor. . . . Abstractedly he said, 'The fewer involved, the more to each share.'

'Share? Oh—I suppose you mean gold.'

Lloyd asked what else he could mean. Franck paused, turned to face the other man. 'For thirty-odd years,' he said, 'I have carried on my researches here in practical alchemy . . . or, rather, certain aspects of it. The field is a vast one, infinitely vast. Money hasn't tempted me, fame hasn't beckoned to me, defeat and failure have not discouraged me, and success has not distracted me.'

But his new partner seemed not to care very much for those observations. His eyes had gone past the speaker. 'What's in there?' he asked, gesturing. 'Up the ladder—'

'In there is where I do most of my work on the alcahest. But it is far from completed.'

Lloyd walked over to the side of the vat. 'The alcahest? Oh, yes. . . .' He climbed the few rungs of the iron ladder. 'For a moment I couldn't think. . . .' He peered over the top of the vat. '"Alcahest" is another one of the names for the Philosopher's Stone, isn't it?'

'No,' said Franck, 'it's another one of the names for the Universal Solvent.' He put the heel of his hand against Lloyd's crotch and pushed up, swiftly and powerfully. There was a splash.

He reached the top of the ladder and peered in, just in time to see the last of Lloyd disappear like a long fade-out in an old-fashioned movie.

Franck sighed. 'So many years . . . so much work . . . so many interruptions . . . no wonder it is so far from complete, and dissolves only organic matter. Sometimes I am tempted to venture into the realm of the philosophical alchemists, and say that only Death itself is the Universal Solvent. . . .' He sighed again, looked into the tank's shimmering liquid. Then he slowly climbed down.

'Drain and sift,' he muttered, opening a valve. 'Drain and sift is the way it goes. Teeth fillings, shoe nails, coins, keys. Sometimes I wonder if it will *ever* consume the inorganic. Of course, if it does, it will eat through the vat and perhaps consume *me*. . . .' The fluid gurgled placidly. 'Oh, it's a weary quest indeed, but at least I'm not spending my time seeking the Philosopher's Stone. Gold-grubbers!' he said, with infinite disdain. 'Snoopers! Vultures! Jackals!'

The Tail-Tied Kings

He brought Them water, one by one.

"The water is sweet, One-Eye," said a Mother. "Very sweet."

"Many bring Us water," a second Mother said, "but the water you bring is sweet."

"Because his breath is sweet," said a third Mother.

The One-Eye paused, about to leave. "I would tell you of a good thing," a Father said, "which none others know, only We. I may tell him, softly, in his ear, may I not?"

In his corner, Keeper stirred. A Mother and a Father raised their voices. "It is colder now," They said. "Outside: frost. A white thing on the ground, and burns. We have heard. Frost." Keeper grunted, did not move. "Colder, less food, less water, We have heard, but for Us always food, always water, water, food, food . . ." They went on. Keeper did not move.

"Come closer," said the Father, softly. "I will tell you of a good thing, while Keeper sleeps." The Father's voice was deep and rich. "Come to my mouth. A secret thing. One-Eye."

"I may not come, Father," said the One-Eye, uncertainly. "Only to bring water."

"You may come," said a Mother. Her voice was like milk, her voice was good. "Your breath is sweet. Come, listen. Come."

Another Father said, "You will be cold, alone. Come among Us and be warm." The One-Eye moved his head from side to side, and he muttered.

"There is food here and you will eat," the other Father said. The One-Eye moved a few steps, then hesitated.

"Come and mate with me," said the milk-voiced Mother. "It is my time. Come."

The One-Eye perceived that it was indeed her time and he darted forward, but the Keeper blocked his way.

"Go, bring water for Them to drink," said Keeper. He was huge.

"He has water for Us now," a Mother said, plaintively. "Stupid Keeper. We are thirsty. Why do you stop him?"

A Father said, "He has water in his mouth which he has brought for Us. Step aside and let him pass. Oh, it is an ugly, stupid Keeper!"

"I have water in my mouth which I have brought for Them," the One-Eye said. "Step aside and—" He stopped, as they burst into jeers and titters.

The Keeper was not even angry. "There was nothing in your mouth but a lie. Now go."

Too late, the One-Eye perceived his mistake. "I may sleep," he muttered.

"Sleep, then. But go." Keeper bared his teeth. The One-Eye shrank back, and turned and slunk away. Behind him he heard the Mother in her milk-voice say, "It was a stupid One-Eye, Father."

"And now," the Father said. The One-Eye heard their mating as he went.

Sometimes he had tried to run away, but everywhere there were others who stopped him. "It is a One-Eye, and too far away. Go to your place, One-Eye. Go to your duty, bring water for the Mothers and Fathers, take Their food to the Keeper, go back, go back, One-Eye, go back," they cried, surrounding him, driving him from the way he would go.

"I will not be a One-Eye any longer," he protested.

They jeered and mocked. "Will you grow another eye, then? Back, back: it is The Race which orders you!" And they had nipped him and forced him back.

Once, he had said, "I will see the goldshining!"

There was an old one who said, "Return, then, One-Eye and I will show you the goldshining on the way." And the old one lifted a round thing and it glittered gold. He cried out with surprise and pleasure.

Then, "I thought it would be bigger," he said.

"Return, One-Eye, or you will be killed," the old one said. "Outside is not for you. Return . . . Not that way! That way is a death thing. Mark it well. *This* way. Go. And be quick—there may be dogs."

There was some times a new one to instruct, blood wet in the socket, at the place of water, to drink his fill and then fill his mouth and go to the Fathers and Mothers, not to swallow a drop, to learn the long way and the turnings, down and down in the darkness, past the Keeper, mouth to mouth to the Fathers and Mothers. Again and again.

"Why are *They* bound?" a new one asked.

"Why are *we* half-blinded? It is The Race which orders. It is The Race which collects the food that other One-Eyes bring to Keeper, and he stores it and feeds Them."

"Why?"

They paused, water dripping from above into the pool. *Why?* To eat and drink must be or else death. But why does The Race order Fathers and Mothers to be bound so that they cannot find their own food and water? "I am only a stupid One-Eye. But I think the Fathers and Mothers would tell me . . . There was mention of a secret thing . . . The Keeper would not let me listen after that . . ."

"That is a big Keeper, and his teeth are sharp!"

Water fell in gouts from overhead and splashed into the pool. They filled their mouths and started down. When he had emptied the last drop in his mouth he whispered, "Mother, I would hear the secret thing."

She stiffened. Then she clutched at him. The other Fathers and Mothers ceased speaking and moving. At the entrance the Keeper sat up. "What is it?" he called. There was alarm in his voice, and it quavered.

"A strange sound," said a Father. "Keeper, listen!" Then—"Slaves?" he whispered.

The Keeper moved his head from side to side. The Fathers and Mothers were all quite still. "I hear nothing," Keeper said, uncertainly.

"Keeper, you are old, your senses are dulled," the deep-voiced Father said. "We say there is a strange noise! There is danger! Go and see—go now!"

The Keeper became agitated. "I may not leave," he protested. "It is The Race which orders me to stay here—"

Fathers and Mothers together cried out at him. "The Race! The Race! We are The Race! Go and find out the danger to Us!"

"The One-Eye—where is the One-Eye? I will send him!" But they cried that the One-Eye had left (as, indeed, one of them had), and so, finally, gibbering and muttering, he lumbered up the passageway.

As soon as he had left, the milk-voiced Mother began to caress and stroke the One-Eye, saying that he was clever and good, that his breath was sweet, that—

"There is no time for that, Mother," she was interrupted. "Tell him the secret. Quick! Quick!"

"Before you were made a One-Eye and were set apart to serve Us, with whom did you first mate?" she asked.

"With the sisters in my own litter, of course."

"Of course . . . for they were nearest. And after that, with the mother of your own litter. Your sire was perhaps an older brother. After that you would have mated with daughters, with aunts . . ."

"Of course."

The Mother asked if he did not know that this incessant inbreeding could eventually weaken The Race.

"I did not know."

She lifted her head, listened. "The stupid Keeper is not returning yet. Good . . . It is so, One-Eye. Blindness, deafness, deformation, aborting, madness, stillbirths. All these occur from time to time in every litter. And when flaw mates with flaw and no new blood enters the line, The Race weakens. Is it not so, Fathers and Mothers?"

They answered, "Mother, it is so."

The One-Eye asked, "Is this, then, the secret? A Father told me that the secret was a good thing, and this is a bad thing."

Be silent, They told him, and listen.

In her milk-rich voice the Mother went on, "But *We* are not born of the same litter, *We* are not sib, not even near kin. From time to time there is a choosing made of the strongest and cleverest of many litters. And

out of these further selections. And then a final choosing
—eight, perhaps, or ten, or twelve. With two, or at most,
three males to be Fathers, and the rest females. And these,
the chosen of the best of the young, are taken to a place
very far from the outside, very safe from danger, and a
Keeper set to guard them, and One-Eyes set apart to
bring them food and water . . ."

A Father continued the story. "It is of Ourselves that
We are talking. They bound Us together, tied Us tightly
with many knots, tail to tail together, so that it was impossible to run away. We had no need to face danger
above, no need to forage. We had only to eat, to drink,
to grow strong—and you see that we are far larger than
you—and to mate. All this as The Race has ordered."

"I see . . . I did not know. This is a good thing, yes.
It is wise."

The Mothers and Fathers cried out at this. "It is not
good!" They declared. "It is not wise! It is not right! To
bind Us together when We were young and unknowing
was well, yes. But to keep Us bound now is not well. We,
too, would walk freely about! We would see the goldshining and the slaves, not to stay bound in the dim-
ness here!"

"One-Eye!" They cried. "You were set apart to serve
Us—"

"Yes," he muttered. "I will bring water."

But this was not what They wanted of him. "One-
Eye," They whispered, "good, handsome, clever, young,
sweet-breathed One-Eye. Set Us free! Unloose the knots!
We cannot reach them, you can reach them—"

He protested. "I dare not!"

Their voices rose angrily. "You must! It is The Race
which orders! We would rule and We will rule and you
will rule with Us!"

". . . . mate with Us!" In his ear, a Mother's voice. He shivered.

Again, they spoke in whispers, hissing. "See, One-Eye, you must know where there are death places and food set out which must not be eaten. Bring such food here, set it down. We will know. We will see that Keeper eats it, when he returns. Then, One-Eye, then—"

Suddenly, silence.

All heads were raised.

A Father's deep voice was shrill with fear. "That is smoke!"

But another Father said, "The Race will see that no harm comes to Us." And the others all repeated his assurance. They moved to and fro, in Their odd, circumscribed way, a few paces to each side, and around, and over each other, and back. They were waiting.

It seemed to the One-Eye that the smoke grew thicker. And a Mother said, "While We wait, let Us listen for Keeper and for the steps of those The Race will send to rescue Us. Meanwhile, you, One-Eye, try the knots. Test the knots, see if you can set Us free."

"What is this talk of 'try' and 'test' and 'see'?" a Father then demanded. "He has only to act and it is done! Have We not discussed this amongst Ourselves, always, always? Are We not agreed?"

A second Mother said, "It is so. The One-Eye has freedom, full freedom of movement, while We have not; he can reach the knots and We can not. Come, One-Eye. Act. And while you set Us free, We will listen, and when We are free, We will not need to wait longer for Keeper and the others. Why do they not come?" she concluded, querulous and uncertain.

And they cried to him to untie Them, set Them free,

and great things would be his with Them; and, "If not," They shrilled, "We will kill you!"

They pushed him off and ordered him to begin. The smell of the smoke was strong.

Presently he said, "I can do nothing. The knots are too tight."

"We will kill you!" they clamored. "It is not so! We are agreed it is not!" And again and again he tried, but could do nothing.

"Listen, Mothers and Fathers," the milk-voiced one said. "There is no time. No one comes. The Race has abandoned Us. There must be danger to them; rather than risk, they will let Us die and then they will make another choosing for new Mothers and Fathers."

Silence. They listened, strained, snuffed the heavy air.

Then, screaming, terrified, the others leaped up, fell back, tumbling over each other. A Mother's voice—soft, warm, rich, sweet—spoke. "There is one thing alone. Since the knots will not loose, they must be severed. One-Eye! Your teeth. Quickly! Now!"

The others crouched and cringed, panting. The One-Eye sank his teeth into the living knot, and, instantly a Father screamed and lunged forward, cried stop.

"That is pain!" he whimpered. "I have not felt pain before, I cannot bear it. Keeper will come, the others will save Us, The Race—"

And none would listen to the Mother.

"Mother, I am afraid," the One-Eye said. "The smoke is thicker."

"Go, then, save yourself," she said.

"I will not leave without you."

"I? I am part of the whole. Go. Save yourself." But still he would not, and again he crept up to her. They came at last to the end of the passage. They could not count the full number of the dead. The smoke was gone now. The Mother clung to him with her fore limbs. Her hind limbs dragged. She was weak, weak from the unaccustomed labor of walking, weak from the trail of thick, red blood she left behind from the wound which set her free.

"Is this outside?" she asked.

"I think so. Yes, it must be. See! Overhead—the goldshining! The rest I do not know," the One-Eye answered.

"So that is the goldshining. I have heard—Yes, and the rest, I have heard, too. Those are the houses of the slaves and there are the fields the slaves tend, and from which they make the food which they store up for Us. Come help me, for I must go slowly; and we will find a place for Us. We will mate, for We are now The Race." Her voice was like milk. "And our numbers will not end."

He said, "Yes, Mother. Our numbers will not end."

With his single eye he scanned Outside—the Upper World of the slaves who thought themselves masters, who, with trap and terrier and ferret and poison and smoke, warred incessantly against The Race. Did they think that even this great slaughter was victory? If so, they were deceived. It had only been a skirmish.

The slaves were slaves still; the tail-tied ones were kings.

"Come, Mother," he said. And, slowly and painfully, and with absolute certainty, he and his new mate set out to take possession of the world.

Paramount Ulj

It was the Russians' own fault that they had picked
that particular week to stage another walkout from the
U.N. And, of course, all the Delegates of all the Peoples'
Democracies had trotted obediently out behind them.
Later on, the Outer Mongolians were to claim that
Things Would Have Been Different If—

But that is very doubtful.

The vessel was spotted first from a fire observation
tower in Yosemite, but by the time the United States
government had begun to act, the visitors had made a
second landing—in Central Park. For a while, it was
believed that there were two ships, but gradually it
came to be realized that there was only one, that it had
shown up in New York City as near instantaneously
after vanishing from California as made no difference.

Prince Prhajhadiphong of Thai, his country's Perma-
nent Delegate, was enjoying his usual morning stroll
when he rounded a corner in the path and saw the two
visitors emerging from the charcoal-colored oval.

"Sunshine," said one of them to the Prince, who could
never afterward recall which, an understandable lapse,

since they were identical twins. H.H. the P.D. was always rather a wag, and it was only with a strong effort that he restrained himself from saying, "Moonshine," in reply to the uncommon greeting.

"And Sunshine to you," he said, bowing. The two men had kumquat-colored complexions, their Lifebuoy-pink hair was worn in a double loop over the right ear, and their clothes glittered and tinkled.

"Are you a person of consequence?" asked one, speaking as if he had (so the Prince thought to himself) a mouthful of hot rice.

"Oh, of very small consequence," the Prince murmured.

The second one observed, in what seemed an approving manner, "You are evidently using the Modest Opposite. If you were indeed what you say, then you would use the Assertive Opposite to aggrandize yourself." He turned to his twin. "Very early evidence of *ovlirb-tav,* eh, Smottleb?"

But Smottleb demurred. "Perhaps, Cumpaw, although he uses the Modest Opposite, it may be that he does so only to confuse us into thinking that he is *really* only of a small consequence. Which would be no evidence at all of *ovlirb-tav,* would it?"

Smottleb considered this. Then he said, "Well, we must find out." They turned to the patient Thai and said in unison, "Take us to your Paramount Ulj."

"Certainly," said Prince Prhadjhadiphong.

As he led the way to a taxi, he reminded himself that, as one who had spent a year in Bangkok's best Buddhist monastery, he should ever reflect that all is *Maya,* or illusion; and that *Maya* can take any form at all.

The hastily created U.N. Committee to Welcome Inter-

stellar Visitors consisted of American Ambassador Stuyvesant Lowell Lee, Dr. Mithra Parseebhoee of India, and
—of course—the Prince himself.

"Which one of you is Paramount Ulj?" asked Cumpaw
(or perhaps it was Smottleb).

"Hm," said the Prince, coughing delicately. "We three
are temporarily exercising the functions of the Paramount
Uljency. You may confide in us."

"Ah, you have not yet held Ordeal and Combat to
select the late Paramount's successor, I assume. Well,
well . . . I share your darkness. Was the deceased a man
of good taste?" Smottleb asked (unless it was Cumpaw).

"Very," said the Prince, as his colleagues hesitated.

"Good. Then let us recline and talk," one visitor said,
"of our Purpose here."

Their devotion to the cause of *ovlirb-tav* can be gauged
by the fact that Earth was the sixty-first planet the twins
had visited—and of the other sixty, only two had shown
a sufficient grasp of this principle, which alone separates
Man from the beasts.

"How to define this term?" one of them wondered
aloud. "Politeness? Decency? Know-how? Civilization?"

"If you have it," the other said, "we share with you.
Everything. We will have but one placenta, your peo-
ple and ours—if you show *ovlirb-tav*. And if not, *pusht!*
You may continue to cook in your own—"

Ambassador Lee asked, perhaps incautiously, "And
how is this quality shown?"

He was informed that this would be learned soon
enough. Pandit Parseebhoee suggested that Earth, too,
might have something of value to share.

"Only if you have *ovlirb-tav*," said Smottleb or Cumpaw. "If not—*smersh!*"

Prince P. inquired where their home planet was, and

they loftily told him that it was so far away that even its sun was not known to him.

"Ah, then you must have the Galactic Drive!" the Prince exclaimed. They raised polite eyebrows. He said, "A means of traveling infinitely faster than the speed of light."

"Ho, this primitive device!" one of them said merrily. "No wonder you have not even reached your moon yet. Yop, yop, yop!" he chuckled.

The Indian Delegate whispered to his American colleague, "For Heaven's sake, do not let them see a newspaper or they will know at once that we have neither piety, politeness, *nor* civilization!"

But the ears of the aliens were sharp. "Newspaper?" one inquired. "By all means, let us see one of your newspapers. It may help us."

The three committee members sat in a moody silence while Smottleb and Cumpaw looked through the morning paper.

"*'Teen-ager Slays Six With Pogo-Stix'—*"

Stuyvesant Lowell Lee sweated, slumped.

"Ah, this shows mettle and fettle, eh, Cumpaw?"

Lee wiped his face on his sleeve, sat up.

"*'Caste Riots in Bombay,'*" the visitor continued. His tone this time was not pleased.

The Pandit hid his eyes in his hand.

"You see, Smottleb: even here. I tell you it is the fault of the uterine aunts; they neglect their duties to the septs. I warned them at home after the *last* caste riots—" the Pandit dropped his hand, and, for a moment, was tempted to buff his fingernails—"but no, they wouldn't listen. Make the uterine aunts responsible for all property damage and you will see a change. *Pusht*, yes!"

They took up the paper again. "'*Coup in Thailand. Pibbulphumphit ousts Pibbulpharphel.*'"

Prince P.'s bright face went impassive.

"Ordeal and Combat for some territorial Ulj," the visitor said indifferently, turning to another story. The Prince smiled, though a bit wanly. And suddenly there was a sound like the trilling of birds.

"Smottleb here," said Smottleb, putting his finger in one ear and seeming to listen. A startled look came over his face. "We shall return at once," he said. The two rose, spoke briefly in an alien tongue.

"Bad news?" inquired one of the U.N. Delegates solicitously.

"Our Paramount Ulj is dead."

The Thai said that he shared their darkness.

"And well you may; he was our father," Smottleb said. The three murmured condolences.

"Will you be back after the funeral?" Ambassador Lee asked.

The twins said they hoped to.

The Prince asked, "Do you practice cremation or burial?"

As neither answered, Pandit Parseebhoee inquired, "Or perhaps you expose your, ah, loved ones?"

Smottleb and Cumpaw looked at each other.

"*Pusht!*" said one.

"*Smersh!*" said the other.

They folded their arms and vanished.

By the time the car arrived in Central Park, there was no trace of the alien ship except a large crowd milling around and craning their necks at an empty sky, and several policemen who repeated over and over again, "Cmahn, cmahn, keep awfadagrass . . ."

The American and Indian Delegates moaned simultaneously, "But what did we *say?*" Not even the usually cheerful Thai had anything to suggest.

The New Paramount Ulj greeted the twins on their return. "Sunshine . . . Nice of you to come back and all that."

"It was nothing. We congratulate you," said the brothers.

The Paramount shrugged deprecatingly. "It was a lucky thrust through the spleen."

The brothers clapped their hands admiringly. "We could not have wished a better death for our father," they said in ritual.

Arm in arm with his successor, they went in for dinner. As they took seats, he said, "Well, and how was this mission? Any luck? Any signs of *ovlirb-tav?*"

"Signs, yes," said Smottleb, "but little more. Do you know, some of them expose their dead?"

There was a general shaking of heads around the high table at this revelation.

"And what is more," Cumpaw confided, "others practice cremation."

The new Paramount said a trifle stiffly, "We can discuss that after dinner, if you don't mind."

But his predecessor's son continued, as if eager to unburden himself, "And the rest of them, if you'll credit me, actually bury their beloved dead!"

There was a stifled shriek and the Dowager Concubine-Uljess was led away by two slave-girls, her napkin pressed tightly to her mouth. Just then, the Gentlemen-in-Waiting arrived with the food. All the guests fell to with good appetite. The late Paramount Ulj had been an old man, but he had always kept himself in good condition and—as everyone assured his proud sons—he was in excellent taste.

A Bottle Full of Kismet

There are no things so outlandish but what someone will collect them with zeal. The field of Chinese snuff-flasks is, however, both respectable and expensive. Hardin Trasker had many of them, though not so many as he would like, and one such item proved most unexpectedly to contain a djinn (non-Chinese). The djinn, released, made his way out into the open air into movement reminiscent of those little things which, touched by a match on the Fourth of July, produced snakes. Only much, much quicker. Hardin Trasker's eyes could scarcely catch the picture, it was all so quick. No sooner was the djinn erect and man-shaped, it promptly offered to sell him a rug.

"Nice Kermanshah?" it said, temptingly . . . in fact, mincingly. "It's a *lovely* little thing. No? Well, then, we must put on our wee thinking caps, mustn't we? Hasheesh? Halvah? Feelthy peectures?" It put its finger against its nose and winked and tittered.

"What the hell *is* this?" demanded Trasker, perplexed and annoyed. "Whoever heard of a djinn peddling rugs? I never heard of an Armenian djinn. Or a swishy djinn.

For that matter, I never even heard of a swishy Armenian. Explain yourself."

"*Must* you think in stereotypes? As a matter of fact," said the djinn, "I am none of these things. What is your objection to a little free enterprise?" Rather sulkily, it drew itself up and folded its arms across its bosom and announced that it was at his service.

After a pause of the barely perceptible sub-variety, it added, "Master," and yawned.

Hardin Trasker was covetous in the extreme. Not for money, but for what money could not buy: in this instance, an object about two inches high, tawny in color, and carved in a profusion of dragons, phoenixes, and other figures out of oriental myth. More about this, later.

Also, he was not a gentleman. Anyone who will tell a charming young woman, who has just proposed a rather jolly housekeeping arrangement, that it is cheaper to buy milk than to—but you know the rest of it—is not a gentleman.

"Keep a *cow!*" she cried, with some measure of fully justified indignation—and then burst out laughing.

"Well, Trasker," she went on, after only just a moment of merriment, "no one can say that you're a mere second-class son of a bitch. I know this fellow, Victor Nielson, he collects those same little whatever-they-are as you do, but they're well, just objects, to him. But with you, Trasker—You really do think more of those damned doo-hickies," she gestured towards the cabinets, "than you do of . . . not just me. Anything. Don't you?"

He nodded. Not in the least ruefully. Smugly, almost. "I won't say that they cost less. Or more," he added, cautiously. "But they're beautiful, they never change, they never give any trouble. It's almost surprising, how you can get caught up in them. Sometimes I even think that I may be a bit irrational on the subject. Do you—"

"Perish the thought," she said, arising. "Well, give me five dollars for the cab, will you?"

He would. "I have your phone number," he said, as she opened the door.

"Yes, but don't bother to call it."

He shrugged, and went back to his treasures, having made a little note of Victor Nielson's name.

"No I don't mind at all your looking at them. As long as *you* don't mind my running you right in and right out, more or less. I've got this appointment, or I'd—"

"Quite all right. Very kind of you as it is."

"—only you called and said you were just in town briefly, Mr. . . . Degman?"

"Degler. Claude Degler. Yes."

Victor Nielson was a pleasant-faced, well set-up young man. His caller was somewhat older.

"Here they are, then. I hope you're not too disappointed. You see, I don't really collect Chinese snuff-bottles—or any other kind, for that matter. I just keep them around because they're decorative, I guess. They're among the few things of my uncle's I *have* kept on, but he didn't really collect them, either: he just *had* them. As a matter of fact," said Victor Nielson, with a hearty laugh, "he collected feelthy peectures."

"Anyway, the snuff-bottles were appraised along with everything else, and the appraiser said they weren't very good, weren't worth very much."

He pointed them out on their shelves. This one was jade, this one was soapstone, this was glass, so was this, and this one—he laughed again. "Well, you know more about it than I do, since you really do collect them. I forget what this is. How did you happen to hear about mine?"

Mr. Degler, as he called himself, quite improperly, smiled in absent wise, gave a little shrug.

"Oh . . . word gets around, you know. . . . This one? This one is lacquer." His face at these words, if one were attending closely, seemed to grow longer and paler, and he held onto the little object in his hand as if for support. Victor Nielson, however, was not attending closely to anything very much except the clock. Being a well-mannered person and fearing to embarrass his guest by this, he grew a bit talkative.

The appraiser had said that this one, the lacquer one? was the least valuable of them all, he said it would barely run to two figures. Nielson hadn't the slightest idea where his uncle had gotten it or the rest of them, unless it was part of the other stuff he had inherited from his and Nielson's late conjoint cousin, Mrs. Bessie, including the money.

"Although I don't even know where she would have gotten them, or why. All she did was sit around and eat candy and stuff."

"Money?" the caller asked, vaguely.

"Yes," said Victor Nielson. "He had this rotten little job in the clearing house and then lazy Julia died and he got it all. All the money, all the stuff. Then *he—*"

His visitor replaced the lacquer object and smiled stiffly. "I must be going now," he said. "Thank you for showing me the things."

"Not at all. Not at *all*. Wish we both had the time for a good long talk about them," he said, with eager insincerity. "Fascinating things, I guess. If you know about them, I mean, I never even knew that the Chinese *took* snuff, I thought they drank tea or something. Drop around again some time!"

Later, and not much later, that night, Hardin Trasker sat in his own apartment intently examining the little item he had just burgled from the apartment of Victor Nielson, who would probably never miss it. It was flattish and flasklike and the predominant color was a cinnabar-red, carved into bas-relief against a dusty gray background. Along top and bottom ran the familiar Grecian frieze pattern. In between and on both sides were a multitude of tiny men in robes and with shaven skulls. Several of them were holding objects which, to the casual eye, seemed to be flails or fly-whisks or maybe even gigantic wishbones. At and rounding one end was a large cat-like animal with pointy ears and a stupid smile; at and rounding the other end was something quite different: imagine, if you can, a sort of great flying frog with affinities to a dragon. One of the little shave-pates seemed to be cowering away from it.

It was all very curious and elliptical. And a little bit battered.

"Yes. . . ." said Trasker, drawn-out and to himself. Then, "Those fools, the appraisers! All they know is what prices collections bring at auctions to settle estates!"

Trasker held one of the two snuff-bottles of that Chang Yu-chuan about whom several curious tales were told at the court of the Empress Dowager.

Had you or had I attempted to open it, we should perhaps have taken long or given up in failure, but Trasker knew that the top did not come off the way we might expect it to; what was more, he knew that way it *did* come off. And in half an instant more the djinn appeared and the brief conversational scene ensued which is recorded at the start of our story.

"Well," Trasker said, judiciously, "It is no more surprising that you should be in a snuff-bottle than in any other kind of a bottle, I suppose. I am sure the story of how you came to be there and all the adventures you have had is very interesting, but let's get down to business. What can you do for me?"

The djinn attempted once again to do a little private trading on his own, accepted the curt rebuff with a brief, philosophical smile; indulged in word-pictures and oriental hyperbole; finally talked turkey. "I can do you a tangible, specific thing," he said. "Something possessing ordinary physical limits. No eternal life. No the-most-beautiful-girl-in-the-world. I mean, that's a purely subjective opinion, wouldn't you agree?"

Trasker waved aside his agreement or disagreement. "What I want is tangible and specific enough," he said. "I want the *other* snuff-bottle of Chang Yu-chuan."

"Of who?" the djinn inquired, politely.

His master repeated the name, adding, "He was third assistant Chief Eunuch at the Imperial Court."

"Oh, *him!*" said the djinn, with a leer and a filthy snigger. He yawned, waved his hand limply. "Well, where is it?"

Informed that it was part of the nonpareil collection of a Mr. Edward Finlayson, Jr., of such-and-such a number, Beekman Place, the djinn nodded, flickered, held out his hand with a something in it.

"What, gone and returned already?" Trasker was astonished. His expression of anticipated pleasure almost at once was replaced by annoyance. "This isn't it!" he cried. "Listen," he said, after a moment. "Let me describe it to you carefully. It is made out of hornbill, the bony beak of a tropical bird. It is about this big . . . a beautiful, a lovely shade of yellow-brown . . . it is carved very

intricately, exquisitely, with three dragons, three phoenixes, and three goblins or demons. It—"

The djinn, who had, rather impatiently, nodded again,
flickered again, and, with slightly raised eyebrows, once
again proffered the contents of his palm.

"No, no, *no!*" cried Trasker, quite enraged. "*Hornbill!*
Not brown jade: *hornbill!*"

The djinn, during this outburst, had been petulantly
examining his long fingernails, and now said, "Well,
really . . . At this rate we shall be here all *night*. I am
supposed to provide service, not expert knowledge in
just any simply arcane field which strikes your fancy.
Come. I tell you what. I shall transport you there, you
make your selection yourself. Then—"

"Done!" exclaimed Hardin Trasker. He takes the outstretched hand. It is as hot as fire to the touch. Instantly he finds himself elsewhere, in a large room furnished with quiet and costly good taste. On glass shelves
illuminated from behind translucent panels stand arrayed
at least one hundred beautiful and priceless Oriental
snuff-bottles. The djinn is nowhere to be seen.

Exercising great restraint, Trasker does not allow his
eyes to linger, and in a few seconds he observes the very
item he had so long coveted. A door opens, he thrusts
his find into his pocket, and turns to face a tall, thin-
faced man, who curiously enough, has his hand in *his*
pocket.

"Oh, now," this man says, "you haven't come here to
admire *snuff-bottles*. How did you get in? Silly question.
Gertrude let you in, of course. Well," he says, with a
sigh of resignation, "she can't say I didn't warn her."
The hand which he takes from his pocket has a gun in it.

A gentleman whose name is of no consequence to this
narrative sat in an over-stuffed chair in an overfurnished

room fiddling with something or other. "Extraordinary,"
he said aloud, "what can be picked up for a few dollars
in these little shops which buy odds and ends of estates.
It is so very hard to resist them." His hand moved indul-
gently, pleasurably among his purchases. "An onyx egg.
A pewter pounce-box. A medallion from the Army of
the Shenandoah. A Chinese—I suppose it is Chinese—
ahh . . ."

The top came off with a final twist and a final tug, and
out poured the djinn. "Now, *you* appear to be a gentleman who would appreciate a bargain," it said, in a con-
fiding tone of voice. "Would you like to buy a nice, *nice*
Kermanshah carpet? No? Hasheesh? Halvah? Feelthy
peectures? *Beautiful* hornbill snuff-bottle?"

The Goobers

When I was a boy I lived for a while after my folks both died with my grandfather and he was one of the meanest, nastiest old men you'd ever want to know, only you wouldn't've wanted to've known him. He had a little old house that there was nothing in the least cute or quaint about and it smelled of kerosene and bacon grease and moldy old walls and dirty clothes. He must've had one of the largest collections of tin cans filled up with bacon grease around there in those parts. I suppose he was afraid there might be a shortage of this vital commodity some day and he was sure as Hell going to be prepared for it.

The dirty old kitchen had two stoves, one wood and one kerosene, and although the thicket out behind the house had enough dead brush and timber in it to heat the place for years he was too damned lazy to swing an axe. Same thing with the clothes. Rather than pay a woman to do a laundry or perish forbid he should actually do it himself, he just let the clothes accumulate and then he'd go through it and use the least dirty ones all over again. Finally every so often it would get so bad that none of the other kids wanted to sit next to me and the teacher'd talk to the neighbors and then one or the other of them who happened to have a gasoline power washing-machine of the old-fashioned sort would come by with one of her kids and a wagon and a couple of bushel baskets.

"I don't know how you let things get into such a condition, Mr. Harkness," she'd say, wrinkling up her nose and breathing through her mouth. "You load these things up and I'll wash'm for you, for pity's sake, before they *fester* on you! You'll both wind up in the *pest* house before you know it. Mercy!"

And the old turd would hobble around trying to look debilitated when actually he was as limber as a black-snake when he wanted to be, frowning and making motions at me to get busy and trot the clothes out, and all the while he'd be whining things like, "I sure do thank you, Miz Wallaby . . ." or whatever in the Hell her name was, "I don't know what we'd do without our neighbors, as the Good Book says. I'm just a poor sick old man and this Boy is too much for me, it's not right I should have such a burden thrust upon me in the decline of my life, I haven't got the strength for it, no I haven't ma'am, he'll be the death of me I predict, for he won't work and he won't listen and he won't obey," and so on and so forth.

Then, once she was out of sight and hearing, he'd sit back in his easy chair that had the bottom sprung out of it and he'd smirk and laugh and carry on about how he'd sure gotten the best of that deal, all right.

"Just set and wait long enough and let the word get around and sure enough, Boy, some damn fool will turn up and do the work! Well, I'm willing. Let'm. Good for their souls." And he'd cackle and hee-haw and dribble Apple Twist tobacco juice onto his dirty old moustache.

He had no shame and he had no pride. Send me begging for food. He'd do that, although he had money for the bootlegger. And he'd send me to steal, too. "Don't tell me you don't want to, Boy. It's the easiest thing there is. You got that big old hole in your overcoat pocket, alls you got to do, Boy, is just drop in a can of pork'n-beans or a box a sardines, let 'm fall into the lining, then just walk out as easy as you please with your two hands in plain sight. Boy, your two hands in plain sight. So don't tell me you don't *want* to, Boy. You want to *eat*, don't you?"

He had it all figured out. It was a perfectly good sort of thing to steal from the A & P, because the A & P was a monopoly. And it was a perfectly good thing to steal from Ah Quong, because Ah Quong was a Chinaman. "Live on a fish-head and handful of rice a day, Boy, and that's the reason us Americans can't compete with 'm."

He talked this way all around town and one day when I was "shopping" in the E Light Grocery Store, old Ah Quong waved me over. I was so afraid, I almost messed myself. I was sure old Ah Quong was going to brain me with a hatchet, having caught on to me, but all he did was to hand me a package. "You give you gland-fodda," he said. I took it and all but ran.

What was there inside of it but a bag of fish-heads and a bag of rice.

You think he was ashamed?

"By grannies, Boy," he said, running his tongue over his gummy old mouth, "we'll make chowder. Nothing makes a better chowder than fish-heads. Rice is nice, too. Rice is a thing that settles mighty easy on the stomach."

He claimed he'd been wounded in the Spanish and

American War but was cheated out of a pension by the politicians. He claimed he'd been to the Yukon for gold. He claimed he'd been a railroad engineer and he claimed this and that and the other thing, but as I got older I come to realize that they were all lies, just lies. He'd rather work hard at a lie than tell the easy truth. But I was a while in catching on to this.

When I say he was mean, I mean he was *mean*. I don't mean he'd ever actually beat me. He wanted to for sure, he'd almost tremble with eagerness to do it sometimes, pulling at his belt and yelling and swearing. But he was too afraid to, because even though I was only about ten years old I was mighty big for my age and getting bigger all the time, and I had all my teeth, too. He knew that in a few years I'd be big enough to take him on and stamp all over him.

So he'd threaten. Mean, nasty threats. "Won't go to get an old man's medicine just because it's mizzling a few drops," he'd yell—meaning, Won't go pick up my booze when it's raining fit to drown kittens. "I had enough. Boy, hear me now! I've had *enough!* I'm turning you over to the Authorities! The County can take care of you from now on! We'll see how you like it in the orphanage asylum from now on! Water mush three meals a day and the cat-o'-nine-tails if you look down your nose at it. I'm going now, I'm going *now*, do you hear me? To tell'm to come pick you up. . . ."

He bundled himself up and skettered out, rain and all. Of course he was just going to get his pint of moon, but I didn't know that. I spent that night moving from one hiding spot to another, my teeth chattering. And finally fell asleep under the bed.

It was after the Authorities started never coming that he began with other threats. "Boy, I don't know what

I'm going to do with you. Yes, I *do* know. I'm going to sell you, Boy—*I'm going to sell you to the Goobers!*"

Well, I didn't know if the Goobers lived in the next township or if they were the name of a foreign power. All I knew was, they weren't good. If they'd've been good my grandfather would sure've never've mentioned them. Nobody ever heard him threaten to put me with some family which would dress me right and keep me clean and feed me decent, that's for sure. He'd even threatened once to feed me to the hogs—not *our* hogs, we never kept hogs, it would've been too much of a work to slop them —but there were plenty of hogs kept in the town—and everybody knew that hogs have been known to eat children, though of course not of my size and age, just babies, but I didn't know that then.

"What're Goobers?" I asked after a little while. Maybe they could've been a kind of animal, I thought, but in a minute I realized no they couldn't, animals couldn't *buy* anything, they had to be people. Maybe the Goobers was their name—like we were the Harknesses.

"You'll wish you never come to know," was his answer. He made his mean little eyes all small, then he opened them so wide that the whites showed all around and the red under lids. "That's what you'll wish! When I sell you to the Goobers! Which I'll do by the Ever-Living Lord of Heaven and Earth. . . ." He never went to church or said a prayer, mind you and he didn't finish, just sucked in his scabby lower lip and nodded at me.

Maybe they were another kind of Authorities. State, maybe, instead of County. Mr. Smith, Chief Goober of the State . . . ? And of course his helpers. Anyway, whatever it was they might want to buy me for, it couldn't be good. I knew that. But I wanted to know more. So I asked Rodney Sloat. He wasn't friend of mine, I had no friends, but he was a non-enemy at least, and he was known to read books.

"Rodney, is there any such a thing as Goobers?"

He nodded his head. "They live in holes in the ground," he said.

It must've been about ten years ago that all of a sudden it came to me that what he must've been thinking of was, of course, *gophers*—and I spilled my coffee all over myself and scalded my legs. All that time it was a mystery what he had in mind. But right just then, when he told me they lived in holes in the ground, it never occurred to me that this was the thing he meant. *They lived in holes in the ground!* Oh, this was worse than anything ever imagined.

The old dog saw how he'd gotten to me, and it was like the smell of blood. He never let up. It was, Do this, Do that, Don't you dast do this or that, or I'll sell you to the Goobers, sure as I'm alive. . . . And I went about in fear of my life, almost, because although he'd never said that the Goobers would kill me—or even harm me—why, how did I know they wouldn't? *They lived in holes in the ground,* didn't they?

The old man didn't have any friends any more than I had friends, but he had cronies, which was more than I had. One of them was a big ruined old hulk of a man with a long fat face all sunken in the middle and white stubble on it, but two little cumps of black eyebrow like curled-up caterpillars. And his name was Barlow Brook. Never just Barlow and never Brook or Mr. Brook.

I broke a plate.

"Got the dropsy," said Barlow Brook.

Grandfather went into his song and dance. "Barlow Brook, the Boy is a torment to me by day and by night."

"Take the hide off of him."

"I swear, Boy, my patience is running out. There's a show-down coming, do you hear me, Boy? It's coming to that. I won't whip you like Barlow Brook says, nooo. I'm too soft-hearted for that. But I warn you, Boy, and I call Barlow Brook to my witness, unless you mend your ways and mighty quick, I will *sell* you to the Goobers."

Barlow Brook hooked open the door of the cold old dusty wood stove with his foot and spit into it. "George Wolf used to talk about the Goobers." He reached himself a hunk of bread and one of our six hundred cans of bacon grease and smeared it on with his fingers and gobbled at it.

"George Wolf," said my grandfather. "He was a bad one."

"Bad as they come. Used to talk about the Goobers. Remember that girl at George Wolf's?"

"Sassy girl?"

"Sassy as they come. You can't make me, used to say. You ain't my father, used to say. Ain't even married to my mother. Try to catch her, he would. Couldn't do it. Take care, he'd tell her. The Goobers will get hold of you one a these days." Bread crumbs, greasy bread crumbs, coming out of his mouth, but I never missed a word, thick as he was speaking, about the sassy girl at George Wolf's.

Barlow Brook washed down his dinner from the smoky-looking bottle, didn't wipe it or his mouth either.

"She says to him, there ain't no such of a thing as any Goobers. Goobers is peanuts, she says to him. George Wolf, he told her. That's *why* they call'm Goobers, he says, they *look* like that. Only not so small. Not near so small. Got wrinkled old shells on. Dirty yellow colored. Even sometimes a couple of hairs. Watch out, sassy. They'll git ahold of you. George Wolf."

Barlow Brook put his moldering shoes up to the kerosene stove.

"You hear, now, Boy," said my grandfather, smirking at me.

I swallowed. I asked what, what happened to the sassy girl at George Wolf's. A quick, secret look passed between those two evil old men. *Some*thing had happened to her, I knew that. I know it now. And I've got my own idea as to what. But, then . . . When Barlow Brook said, "Came and *got her*," I had no idea except for sure that the Goobers were the *they*.

You can be sure that I did my best not to break any more plates. I fetched and I carried. When my grandfather said "Come here, Boy," I came a running. But he was a bully, and these is no satisfying of bullies. He knew I was in mortal terror of being sold to the Goobers and he never let up. There were hickory trees back in the thicket and one day he sent me to get some nuts. I didn't mind at all and I went quick.

And I came back quick. There was a bad family by the name of Warbank lived outside of town, so bad that even my grandfather didn't want anything to do with them. They were meaner than he was and they had a bunch of big yellow dogs meaner than they were. When I got to the hickory trees with my bucket, there was Ding Warbank and Cut Warbank with their own buckets, and their dogs.

"You get the Hell out of here," said Ding.

"It ain't your thicket," I said.

"Get him," said Cut. The dogs came after me and I ran. One of them got hold of my pants and it came away in his teeth. Behind me, Cut called them back.

"We better not see you here again," yelled Ding.

My grandfather took on fierce. No trashy Warbanks, he yelled, were going to tell him he couldn't have nuts from "his own" thicket.

"You go on back there," he ordered. "Go on, now."

I didn't move.

"Go *on*, I tell you! Go on, go on, go on! You want me to sell you to the Goobers?"

Oh, I was afraid of that, all right. I was afraid of the Goobers. But I'd never really seen any. And I *had* seen those Warbanks' yellow dogs, felt their white shiny teeth pulling that bite out of my pants leg. And I wouldn't go.

He yelled and he raged. Then, all of a sudden, he quit. "All right, Boy," he said. "All right, then. I am through warning you. In one hour's time, as I live and as my name's Dade Harkness, in one hour's time I swear that I will sell you to the Goobers. Now git out my sight— but don't you leave the yard!"

What he figured on, I guess, was that the Warbanks would be gone by then and I'd rush out and get his old hickory nuts and then he'd pardon me . . . for the time being.

I stumbled away. "It's four o'clock," he yelled after me. "They'll be here at five. Don't bother packing—you won't need nothing!"

An hour like that, I never want to pass again. I hid here and hid there, till I was sweaty and dirty as never before. But I didn't trust any place. By and by I got so thirsty that I had to come out and get to the pump. I could hear the old man muttering to himself.

His warning about not leaving the yard didn't matter to me worth a poke of peas—he, well, what could he've done to me for disobeying? Sell me to the Goobers? He was going to do that anyway . . . he said. Of course, he'd said

it before and he'd changed his mind before, too. I knew
only one thing for sure, and that was that I couldn't stand
any more of it. Anything was likely to be better.

I'd never been to George Wolf's place, but I knew
where it was, and it wasn't all that far away. About
a mile or so off, on the old dirt road along the creek.
It was an ugly old shack, never had a lick of paint on it,
I guess, though I barely noted that any more than I did
the broken windows or the roof falling in on one side and
the weeds and underbrush choking up the front yard.

If George Wolf had been the original local acquaint-
ance of the Goobers, then the Goobers couldn't've lived
too far away from his place. That was the way my
thoughts were running—and I was running, too—right
into the woods and down the hill and almost into the
swamp that stopped me going further.

"Goobers!" I yelled. "Goobers! You old Goobers! You
hear me?" I screamed.

There was nothing but the echo of my voice. It was
darkish there, and clammy, and it smelled bad and I
was hot and cold and sweaty and I took a big breath and
went on yelling again.

"I don't care if he sells me! I don't care if you buy
me! He isn't going to go on scaring me like this! You
want to buy me? You just come on and do it!"

Something was buzzing when I stopped again. Maybe
just a dragon fly. Something moved in the gray underbrush. Maybe just the wind. I could see a hole in the
ground not far off. Maybe it was just a plain, ordinary
hole. But I didn't wait to find out about any of this. I
turned and ran and stumbled away.

Where? Why, where but back to the old man's house,
back to the only sort of home I knew. I didn't know

what was going to happen, but I knew it was going to happen there. It had to.

I slowed down to a soft walk before I got to the yard. Probably he didn't even know I'd gone, didn't think I'd've dared to. And I could still hear him muttering to himself for a while. Then, suddenly, he stopped.

So did I. Stopped breathing, I mean. I guess. The bell in the old church was striking, and while I'd missed the start, there was no need for me to count the chimes. It only struck the hours. So it had to be five o'clock.

I darted a quick look at the vines hiding his chair from where I was standing. Chair, no, I couldn't see it. But I could see *him*—see his head, anyway, for he'd gotten up, sort of and had poked his face forward. It had gone the most horrible ugly sort of putty color. His eyes had a glaze over them like cold fried eggs. I had to turn to see what he was looking at, though of course I knew.

There were the Goobers, coming up the back path.

They were under my height. There were three of them and they had dirty yellow colored wrinkled old shells on, with even a few hairs. And dirt was clinging to them.

"Where Boy?" asked the first.

"Here Boy," said the second.

"You sell Boy?" asked the third.

They walked up and squeezed my arms and felt my legs. They pulled on my nose and grabbed hold of my tongue. They spun me around and thumped me on the back. Then they quit.

"No," said the first.

"No good," said the second.

"No buy boy," said the third.

They turned around and walked off. I watched them

go, not even turning around when I heard my grandfather keel over and thump the porch floor.

After that, of course, I made his life a living Hell until I ran off two years later at the age of twelve, and there wasn't a damned thing the old bastard could do about it.

Dr. Morris Goldpepper Returns

James E. (for Elphonsus) Dandy paced the floor of the office of his ranch at Tishomingo, the showplace of the State of Texas (and hence not to be confused with any ranch which might be located in or at Tishomingo, Oklahoma), in a manner which can only be described as restless. From time to time he sought, like Boethius, the consolations of philosophy—using this word in its former interpretation as meaning "science"—from his bookshelf. But for once, the writings of Crowe, Holwager, Barrett, Shields and Williams—not to mention Oliver—for once the writings of these great scientific pioneers failed to either to console or absorb him. His burden was heavy. His need was great. His pace was restless.

Some distance away, exactly how much is unnecessary to state in terms of exact precision, all things (as the great Einstein has taught us) being relative: what counts as a long way in the State of Rhode Island and Providence Plantations is a mere jaunt in Texas . . . some distance away, to continue, a pretty and personable young person of the female persuasion was weeping bitterly. Great tears rolled from her large eyes and down her soft cheeks.

"But Daddy, Daddy, Daddy!" she pled and implored. "None of that is 'Little Jimmy's' fault. Why can't we get married, Daddy, Daddy, please?"

Her name was Mary Jane Crawford. The man whom she addressed in terms of filial allegiance was her father, Dr. Clement (or "Clem") Crawford, a landowner and husbandman; in other words, a rancher; besides holding the *éclat* of a degree in Dental Medicine.

The question instantly and quite properly arises, why was this last fact not mentioned first, and the answer is that Dr. "Clem" Crawford—or "Doc," a familiarity and diminutive which would give justified offense in large centers of populous habitation such as cities, but which in rural areas may be, and often is, used without offense —"Doc Clem" Crawford had for some years given over and retired from active practice of this highly important profession, and had since devoted his time to agriculture and its allied crafts.

"Mary Jane," he said, somewhat testily, "I wish you'd quit all that bawling. I didn't say you couldn't marry 'Little Jimmy', I only said you couldn't marry him *now*. It's not his fault that 'Big Jimmy' got himself into this pickle. But all he's got in this world is his share of whatever his daddy's got, and it looks like there's a powerful big chance his daddy might *lose* whatever he's got. I just couldn't hardly bear to think of my little girl having to rough it, cooped up in some little old ten-room house. 'Course, you could go right on living *here* and 'Little Jimmy' could work for *me*. But no. He's just as bullheaded as his daddy."

Mary Jane went off, disconsolate and unhappy. Her father continued to sit in his chair, as if brooding over his daughter's affairs, but the fact is that he had unwelcome worries of his own.

In the vast kitchen of the Crawford ranch-house a comely woman of middle age was engaged in baking pies of fruits and other delicious comestibles. This was Mrs. Doothit, the housekeeper, a widow-woman, as the local vernacular idiom has it. There had been a time when she felt that she had reason to believe an interest in her existed on the part of her employer, Dr. Clement ("Clem") Crawford—who was a widower—which was separate and apart from such considerations as her flaky and juicy pies, her toothsome steaks, her savory coffee, and delicious roasts . . . though by no means diminished by them.

During this time she thought she was aware of a certain look in her employer's eye, and a certain tone in his voice. But that time had passed, and with it had passed much of Mrs. Doothit's interest in her work. She had even been considering taking a position as housemother in an establishment for underprivileged girls that was maintained in a suburb of Dallas by the Southern Baptist Convention.

But she put off making this decision from day to day.

Upstairs, in the spacious suite of rooms generously put at his disposal by his host, Clement ("Clem") Crawford, DDM (Ret.), was yet another of the *dramatis personae,* or cast of characters, of the narration which we now peruse, namely and videlicet one Morris Goldpepper, Doctor of Dental Surgery, inventor of the Goldpepper Bridge and the Goldpepper Crown, and perfector of the Semi-Retractable Clasp which bears his name. He is as it were, the Livy, Macrobius or Gibbon of this annal. (Modesty, epitomized by my automatic shrinking from the spotlight, obliges me—with this one exception—to cleave to the Third Person previously and henceforth.)

The suite of rooms was a veritable apartment of its
own, consisting of a sleeping chamber, a lounge, an office,
a kitchen, a bar (which Dr. Goldpepper's well-known
temperate habits rendered about as useful as certain mam-
malian appurtenances on a boar), a games-room and
what had previously been another sleeping chamber but
which had been converted at no small cost and effort
into a laboratory for the fabrication and synthesis of
dental prosthetic devices.

All this had been done out of pure generosity, affection
and respect by Dr. Crawford on behalf of his old Navy
Dental Corps "buddy", Dr. Goldpepper.

It is not to be thought that Dr. Goldpepper had sur-
rendered occupancy of his bachelor apartment in the
Hotel Davenport, nor yet of his laboratory on Broadway
in the Upper West 70s, in order to live the life of a
country squire in the sylvan or (considering the sparse-
ness of trees) semi-sylvan fastnesses of John C. Calhoun
County, Texas. The facts of the matter, not altogether
pleasant, are that he was undergoing the long and delicate
process of recuperation intendant upon the aftermaths of
his rescue from the grasp and clutches of the malevolent
inhabitants of a distant planet in another part of the
Galaxy, the captivation and captivity whereon has already
been recorded in these pages; anent which, enough—no
point in chewing a twice-told tale.

At any rate, Dr. Goldpepper rested in his luxuriously
appointed guest quarters. He took long walks around the
ranch, delighted in the verdant greenery of its crops and
the rolling undulation of its hills. And, for the first time
since his boyhood, he recommenced the gentle piscatorial
craft or pastime of angling.

The M Bar L Ranch (named after the Honorable Mi-
rabeau Bonaparte Lamar, sometime President of the Re-

public of Texas, and a boyhood idol of "Doc Clem") was located on the Little Comanche River. To those used to the Majestic Hudson and the navigable East, the application "river" to what others might well deem a mere creek is at first difficult. However that may be, the waters of the Little Comanche teemed with trout, bass and other edible species of fish. Dr. Goldpepper considered himself too impatient to undertake mastery of dry- or even wet-fly fishing, but his efficient host kept his bait box supplied with worms of a most surprising stature or length, and, thus aided, the guest seldom failed to come home with something in his creel besides air.

It was on the day on which our story opened that Dr. Goldpepper returned from a circumambulation of the scenery and was told by his host that someone was waiting to see him.

"Waiting to see *me?*" was his surprised rejoinder. "*Who?*"

"*I* don't know, 'Morry,'" said Doctor "Clem." "Some little old man."

Put completely off guard by his awareness of the Texan habit of placing the words *little* and *old* before almost any odd noun—a "little old baby," "a little old elephant" or "brontosauras"—Dr. Goldpepper was therefore astonished to see that the personage waiting for him was literally little and—to all outward presages—old.

But in another fraction of a second he recognized the typical blue gums in the individual's mouth, open in a fawning sort of false, deceitful smile, and recognized himself to be in the presence of a member of the hideous and alien race whose unwilling captive he had been on far-off Upsilon Centauri (as he had with wry humor denominated it to himself, to avoid becoming embittered).

Startled, Dr. Goldpepper uttered a cry of surprise. Inadvertently he stepped behind "Doc" Crawford, who inquired, "'Morry,' what in the Hell is the matter?"

Goldpepper lashed out fearlessly at the invader with his fishing-rod, but the diminutive alien evaded the blow and groveled on the floor, crying, "Have kindness, Merciful Goldpepper!" and attempted to place his head beneath Goldpepper's foot.

Once it was realized that this was a sign of submission, indeed of homage or obeisance, and not some sort of wrestling hold, the latter at once became calm.

"What is the meaning of this outrageous intrusion?" Dr. Goldpepper demanded, sternly and outraged. "Is it your intention to abduct me yet another time, as if I hadn't had enough *tsuris* already?"

"Assist, assist, Benevolent Goldpepper!" the alien wailed as he writhed on a floor-rug made from the pelts of fifty-four coyotes shot by the owner of the M Bar L. "Forgive, Great Dentist of the Ages!"

Seizing the unwelcome one by the scruff of his collar while he was still attempting his act of vasselage, Dr. Crawford inquired, in some amazement, "Do you mean to tell me, 'Morry,' that this little old thing was one of the gang that kidnapped you?"

"It was not by violence, but by subterfuge," said the erstwhile victim, wearily. "And I don't care to dwell on the subject. Ask him to leave."

"'*Ask*' him?!" Dr. Crawford exclaimed with an oath, opening the door and flinging the intruder out with some measure of violence. He then summoned one of his employees, a tall, dark and ugly man with only one eye, known as 'Ojito' Gonzales, and on whose head there was declared to be in the State of Chihuahua (or it might be Sonora) an unofficial reward of ten thousand pesos. He enjoined the Mexican not to allow the extraterrestrial upon the premises again under pain of severe displeasure.

Much shaken by these events, Dr. Goldpepper allowed himself to be persuaded to take a small glass of Bourbon whiskey, and Mrs. Doothit made him some strong coffee.

While the agitation produced by these untoward events had yet to die down, a sound of an automobile was heard outside in the driveway. Looking out the window, those inside perceived the well-known palomino Cadillac of James E. (for Elphonsus) "Big Jimmy" Dandy. Seated with him was his son "Little Jimmy," a perfect example of hyperbole, or exaggeration not intended to deceive, for it was obvious to the naked eye that "Little" Jimmy was at least six feet six inches tall, and had an open and pleasant face. It was a source of sorrow to Dr. Morris Goldpepper that circumstances beyond his control were providing impediments to the marriage of this young man to Mary Jane Crawford, of whom he was very fond (in an avuncular way, she referring to him as "Uncle Morry").

The young man waved to them and then walked off with his fiancée, who had run out to meet him. His father looked at them, shook his head and walked slowly into the house.

"Howdy, 'Clem,'" he said, in greeting. "Howdy, 'Doc'" —referring to guest, not host.

"Anything new, 'Jimmy'?" Dr. Crawford inquired. As Mr. Dandy slowly shook his head, Dr. Crawford pressed his lips together. Then he rose. "I've got to tend to some business down at the south forty," he said. "You and 'Morry' entertain one another, now. 'Jimmy,' you and your boy stay for dinner, now, hear?" And he disappeared. Plainly, he did not desire an occasion to arise for him and his friend to be alone together, doubtless for fear the subject of the postponed nuptials would be broached.

Doing his best to make conversation, Dr. Goldpepper inquired, "I wonder why people always talk about the *south* forty. How is it that a person seldom if ever hears mention of the *north* forty?"

But Mr. Dandy didn't rise to this intriguing ethno-ecological problem. He merely shook his head in a bemused fashion and said, "G—damn if *I* know, 'Doc.'" And then he sighed.

He was a typical Texas-type rancher: tall, reddened face, boots, Stetson.

He sighed again, looking at a mounted portion of a white-tailed deer which Dr. Crawford had, in rather questionable humor, placed over the mantel of the giant fireplace.

"Mr. Dandy—"

"'Jimmy,' 'Doc.'"

"'Jimmy'—forgive me for intruding on your own personal emotional difficulties, but if you won't mind—after all, although not a physician in the common sense of the word—let alone a psychiatrist, psychologist or psychoanalyst (whether Freudianly oriented or otherwise), still, in the long years of professional duty before I commenced the more solitary work of dental prosthesis, in my civilian practice as well as the United States Navy Dental Corps, I have had patients confide in me all manner of difficulties, and—"

Mr. Dandy groaned aloud. "'Doc,'" he said, "do you know anybody who wants to buy fifteen million earthworms?"

There was a silence.

Dr. Morris Goldpepper was convinced that the man's

mind had snapped, thus causing a mental aberration of no mean proportion.

"How do you mean, 'fifteen million earthworms'?" he inquired, cautiously. Delusions of the most multifarious kinds he had met with before, but this was something new.

"It's all the fault of that G—damn Federal Government," said Mr. Dandy. "If it wasn't for Them, I'd never of gotten in this here predicament. The least they could do is buy 'm off me. They buy surplus wheat, don't they? Butter? Cotton? Goober peas? Why, do you know that last year the Federal Government spent over eight million tax-dollars to keep up the price of lard?"

"What!" exclaimed Dr. Goldpepper, stung to the quick. "With my money?"

Mr. "Big Jimmy" Dandy smacked his right fist into his left palm. "Yes, sir, with your money! And with my money! But can I get some of it back when I need it? No, sir. Them and their G—damn flood control! Why, when I think of it—"

Wistfully, Dr. Morris Goldpepper thought of the perfectly equipped laboratory upstairs, with its neat array of wires of teeth, shellac trays, plaster, dental stone, denture trays, casting ovens and machines, Baldor lathes and Bunsen burners. Here he could have been at work on his favorite project, developing the Goldpepper Cap, instead of listening to the disjointing babblings of some backwoods anti-Federalist. He sighed.

"What is the precise or even approximate connection," he inquired, "between governmental projects for flood control, and the sale or purchase of earthworms?"

The rawboned, rugged rancher looked at him ruefully. "That's right," he said. "You're not from around here. You wouldn't know. Well, 'Doc,' the Federal Government was supposed to start this here flood control project of building dams along the Little Comanche, Big Comanche, Middle Comanche, Muddy Tom, Clear Tom and Bullhead River Valleys, which would provide twenty-seven new lakes. Now, you know, 'Doc,' lakes are pretty scarce in this part of Texas. I don't suppose there's more than one or two a man couldn't, us, spit across, with a favorable wind behind him.

"So you can imagine what twenty-seven new lakes would mean. *Twenty-seven lakes!*"

"Hmm," said Dr. Morris Goldpepper thoughtfully.

Every fisherman in Texas, Mr. "Big Jimmy" declared enthusiastically, would flock to the new Lakes Area, to say nothing of multitudes from other states. It would be the biggest thing since the discovery of oil. "So naturally," he said, "I looked to increase my stock."

"Your stock?"

"Yes. On my ranch."

Dr. Goldpepper, who had been thinking in terms of mutual funds, common and preferred, a subject about which he knew little or nothing, not being a speculator by nature, chuckled gently. "I see," he said. "Black Angus? Santa Gertrudis? Brahmas?"—terms he had acquired from his host, Clement ("Clem") Crawford, D.D.M. (Ret.). "You planned to sell meat to these visiting tourists? Barbecue? Hamburgers?"

Mr. Dandy cast a most peculiar look upon him. "Do you mean to say, 'Doc,'" he inquired, "that you don't know what kind of critters I raise on my ranch?"

In the embarrassed silence which followed they could hear the two young people who were walking by outside. Mary Jane was sobbing all over "Little Jimmy's" silk shirt and had soaked it to a transparency. He was patting her shoulders with his huge hands and saying, "Now, Honey. Now, Honey."

"Er—*what* kind?"

"In Texas, 'Doc,' when they say 'Jim Dandy,' they mean earthworms. And when they say 'earthworms,' they mean 'Jim Dandy.' Simultaneous terms, sir. Simultaneous terms. I started out with one worm tub twenty-five years ago and now I've got the largest worm ranch in the State of Texas! And that means in the world. One square mile of worm pits, 'Doc'—think of that. One square mile of worm sheds, worm tanks and worm boxes." He gazed into the far distances, a proud and dreamy look on his seamed face. "Earl B. Shields—you've heard of Earl B. Shields, everybody's heard of Earl B. Shields—Earl B. Shields devotes two whole chapters to me in *Commercial Earthworm Raising*. George H. Holwager's *Bigger and Better Red Worms* has fifteen illustrations of my ranch. Calls me 'a model for all progressive worm ranchers to follow!' What do you think of *that?* Barrett, Oliver, Crowe, Williams and the others, they all refer to me, yes, sir."

Then the look of exaltation vanished from his rugged features.

"But I raised my sights too far," he said. "It was the mere thought of them twenty-seven lakes and the folks flocking to all of'm that set me off. What a market for bait worms! And me setting right here in the middle of it, astride the main highway! I advertised, took whole pages in the *National Worm Rancher*, offered top prices— eight dollars per five hundred for Giants, five dollars per five hundred for Mediums and four dollars per five hundred for Run-of-the-Pits. Offered purchase agreement guarantees for three years ahead . . ."

In order to house his new stock, the enthusiastic

rancher had erected new buildings. In order to pay for them, he had borrowed.

Alas for the vanity of human wishes! (As Samuel Johnson, Ll.D. (Oxon.) called it.) Alas for ambition!

The Federal Government, in the name of Economy, had canceled the flood control project for the area including the Little Comanche, Big Comanche, Middle Comanche, Muddy Tom, Clear Tom and Bullhead riverine regions—thus leaving "Big Jimmy" Dandy of the Jim Dandy Earthworm Ranch holding, as it were, the bag.

What right (he demanded) had the Federal Government to come messing things up in Texas with Economy? If Texans had wanted Economy (he declared) they'd have stayed a Republic.

"And so here I am," he asseverated, "with fifteen million worms in my pits, and my regular markets can't take no more than a million of 'm. 'Doc,' you see before you a ruined man. My hopes are blasted, my lands are mortgaged and it looks as if 'Little Jimmy' and Mary Jane won't be able to get married for years and years, because I just know my boy wouldn't break his daddy's heart by taking on the responsibility and expense of a wife before his daddy's debts were paid off down to the last copper penny. I'd blow my brains out if I thought otherwise, and he knows it; yes, he does.

"Just the thought of all them hungry beauties crawling and wiggling in my worm pits, and no market a-tall for'm, makes me feel raw and miserable in the pit of my stomach. I wonder if Miz Doothit baked any sweet potato pie lately. Though I'll take rhubarb-pecan if she hasn't."

Doctor Morris Goldpepper declined an invitation to join the rancher in the kitchen, and, on the terminologically inexact plea of a headache, withdrew to take another long walk in the country.

With one part of his mind Dr. Goldpepper mused upon the problem of the Goldpepper Cap, for so many long years his perpetual Work In Progress—should it be, for example, reticulated or non-reticulated?—while simultaneously with another part of his mind he brooded over the question of "Big Jimmy," "Little Jimmy" and Mary Jane.

Almost before he realized it he found himself upon a sort of a high mound or hillock, from whence he had a view of much of the property belonging to his friend Dr. Crawford. Everywhere the green verdure grew—except on the hillock, which was dusty and arid and nourished (if that is not too strong a word) only a handful of sickly weeds.

A scrabbling sort of noise caught his attention, and he turned to observe the identical alien from Upsilon Centauri who had earlier been ejected from the property, in the current act of kneeling and pouring handfuls of dust on his head with both hands.

"Abject I am, Great Goldpepper," he whined. "Abasing myself before you in humility I am. On behalf of my people apology offering, I am. Forgive, forgive, Compassionate Goldpepper!"

At first Doctor Morris Goldpepper resolved to sell his life dearly. But the thought occurred to him that this creature from another galactic quadrant might just conceivably be telling the truth. Furthermore, his curiosity was piqued.

"What are you doing here?" he inquired. "On the terms of the peace treaty signed between your planet, the American Dental Association and the Waterfront Works Union (acting through their representative, Mr. Albert Annapollo, and the Longshoremen's Dental Health Plan—who acted as our shock troops—I was to be released from the captivity wherein I toiled making false teeth to enable your naturally toothless race to pose as Earthmen; and those of you on this planet were to leave *instanta*, on pain of having your planet's water fluoridated without mercy! Therefore I must beg to inquire what you think you are doing here?"

"The slightest trace of fluorine to us instant death is, Life-loving Goldpepper," the alien sniveled. "Have ruth!"

Touched despite himself, Dr. Goldpepper magnanimously directed him to speak without fear. This the non-terrestrian lifeform (his race had two hearts, and six distinct and articulate digits on each hand and foot) proceeded to do so.

"Since you from us taken were, great calamity upon us has come, Auspicious Goldpepper," he moaned. "Assist, assist!"

"What seems to be the trouble?"

"Overpopulation."

Somewhat stiffly, Dr. Goldpepper pointed out that he was not Margaret Sanger.

"Malnutrition! The soil of our home world for cycles, sickening has been. Woe, woe, woe! Our stricken planet aid, Scientific Goldpepper!"

In a *précis*, or nutshell, the story he told was that, as a result of some curious condition of their planet's soil itself, the slith crop, source of their staple gelatinous food, had failed by forty per cent, and was still failing. Purts, the prime source of gruel, had dropped to a mere twenty per cent of normal; and as for sneet, kutch and zooky, the nutritive elements of which were scantier, it was doubtful if the crops would reach maturity. The soil chemists of Upsilon Centauri, who were as advanced, probably, as our own, had pronounced themselves baffled. Large areas had been sprayed with Kz.

Pf. Kz. to no avail, and larger ones irrigated with snurg without the slightest results.

"Once our whole planet like *that* looked," the spokesman wailed. "Now, like *this* it is." He gestured from the greenery on all sides to the sterility of the hill, or undulation, on which they stood; and he stooped to cast more dust on his head.

As Doctor Goldpepper followed his gestures, he observed one of the ranch-hands coming their way, and indicated, by waving his hand, that he desired this man to come up.

"'Doc,' seens you're here," the man said, coming up to him, "I got thishyere tush that's been givin me Hell, my face is all swoll up, and I been livin mostly on beans an beer. See?" And he obtruded a dusty finger into his mouth to indicate the offending canine.

"Come to the ranch-house when you can, where I have my instruments, and I'll take a look at it," said Dr. Goldpepper. "Meanwhile, if you will pardon my curiosity, why is this particular hill so desolate, compared to what I might call the lushness of the rest of the ranch?"

The man withdrew his finger, sucked meditatively on the tooth and then said, "Why, how the land looks hyere, that's how *all* thishyear land use ta look, twell we got in them Jim Dandy Giant Golden-Red Hybrids. Now, evva othuh bit a land hyere is green an growin. We keeps thishyear little old hill seprut jer showin whut it oe'ul use ta look like; will it hurt much, 'Doc'?"

And in this wise was Dr. Morris Goldpepper reminded of the singular and curious ability of the common earthworm—let alone the Jim Dandy Giant Golden-Red Hybrid earthworm—to rejuvenate a piece of ground by moving through it, and by moving *it* through *them*. "Disgusting subject," some might say, but to Dental Science nothing natural is disgusting; thus cogitating, he returned to the ranch-house, followed by the Upsilon Centurian, just in time to catch "Big Jimmy."

America's leading worm rancher was loath to believe that the alien was from another planet, but, upon being assured and reassured that he was not, at any rate, from the Soviet Union, he professed his complete willingness to do business. After all, it is not every day in the week that one finds a customer for fifteen million earthworms.

However, the term "customer" implies not only sale, but purchase as well. Purchase may be by cash, goods or service. Cash, it was obvious, the Upsilonians did not have. The only service of which they were possessed which was at all likely to be of use was that of teleportation (matterproting, according to another usage); and it was agreed that this was something for which the world was not yet prepared. Which left "goods."

The Upsilonian offered, when the crops of his native world should be restored to their former yield, to pay for the worms, pound for pound, in slith, purts, sneet, kutch and/or zooky. But on being informed by Doctor Morris Goldpepper (who had lived on these substances and their derivatives for months) that the best of them tasted like old library paste, Mr. Dandy declined. He also eructated.

"Pardon me, folks," he said, abashed and discomfited. "It's a sort of nervous indigestion, which I get every now and . . . What in thee Hell are *these?*"

"These" were a number of objects in a small box offered by the alien Upsilonian, apparently the same bulk as a five-grain aspirin tablet, but shaped rather like tiny pretzels.

"Minor medications of my planet, they are," he said.

"For ailments of stomach, colon, freest and grunk, good they are. Take, take, Worm-Raising Dandy."

He took, and while he was swallowing, Doctor Crawford asked, "They good for anything else?"

The Upsilonian reflected. "Arthritis," he said, after cogitating thoughtfully. Doctor "Clem" avowed himself an irregular victim to what he thought might be arthritis, in his left knee, and swallowed one of the pillular pretzels before his colleague could point out to him that this was all a non-scientific approach to a highly scientific problem.

It was at this point that "Little Jimmy" came in and reminded his father that they had fifteen million worms to take care of and hence for that reason couldn't stay there all day and all night, much as he ("Little Jimmy") would personally prefer to do. The muffled sound of Mary Jane sobbing outside was audibly heard when he paused, reluctantly.

His father rose. "Boy's right," he posited. "Well, I guess I'll have to come back tomorrow and continue the discussion. I sure do hope we can think of something. Bye." And they drove off in the palomino Cadillac, and then Doctor Goldpepper had to treat the ranch-hand with the infected tooth. It was a root-canal job, but, with the able if reluctant assistance of his colleague, was successfully accomplished.

Everyone retired to bed rather early, including the Upsilonian. "I believe I'll take another one of those doohickeys," the host observed, as he prepared to go upstairs.

"Has your arthritis been bothering you?" Dr. Goldpepper inquired solicitously.

"No; but why take chances?" was the rejoinder. "Night, 'Morry.' Night, Mary Jane. Night, um."

Mary Jane sniffled.

The next morning found Doctor Morris Goldpepper sipping his pink grapefruit juice (from which fruit Texas should be more famous than it is) with only Mary Jane for company; and she had nothing to say except an occasional semi-stifled sob.

Before he had finished the job, the Dandys drove up, Mr. Dandy, Senior, bounding into the breakfast-nook (it was as big as the Grand Ballroom at the Hotel Davenport) with his red face full of beaming joy. "It worked!" he cried—a noise which produced the Upsilonian on the scene. "Big Jimmy" picked him from his feet and danced around the room with him. "It worked! Settled my stomach like it never was settled before! It's just *got* to be good for arthritis, too! I figure half the population of the United States has got nervous stomachs, and the other half has arthritis! Mr. Upsilonian (say, are you Armenian? I've known some real fine Armenians!), I'll take seven and a half million white ones, and seven and a half million pink ones, a worm for a pill. A deal?"

The alien was too startled to do more than nod.

Dr. Crawford came down at that moment. "Mary Jane, honey," he observed, "you trot right out and give your sweetheart a real big good-morning kiss, hear? And tell him that the wedding is *on!*"

The delighted girl rushed, squealing merrily, from the room, and her father, in a lowered tone of voice, winked and dug the other Earthmen in the ribs with his elbows, as he observed, "I found something *else* that those pills are good for! Why, good *morning*, Lilybelle!"

Doctor Goldpepper, on the point of asking *what* else, looked up to see who "Lilybelle" might be, and lo and behold, it was no other one but the comely housekeeper, whom he had never heard "Clem" address other than as

"Mrs. Doothit, ma'am," before. She blushed, and her eyes, before she cast them down, were seen to sparkle.

"Hmm," observed "Big Jimmy," adding, "Well, I guess now we know what 'freest' means. Or maybe it's 'grunk.' Mr. Upsilonian, make that five million white ones, five million pink ones and five million green ones. Tell them factories to start gearing for increased production! Yippay!"

"Ee-yih-hoo!" cried Doctor Crawford.

The alien said nothing, but genuflected and kissed the cuffs of Doctor Goldpepper's trousers.

How Upsilon Centauri was saved from soil sickness and famine, how the Jim Dandy Ethical Drug Company of Texas, Inc., moved with the speed of light into the ranks of the great corporations along with its sister-syndicate, the Jim Dandy Giant Golden-Red Hybrid Earthworm Company; how James E. (for Elophonsus) Dandy, Jr., married Mary Jane Crawford at the same double ceremony which united her father in matrimony to Mrs. Lilybelle Doothit, are matters too profuse in content to be recorded here by Doctor Morris Goldpepper, now restored once again to health and duty; who, desiring only the good and welfare of the American Dental profession and the human race, is glad to go down to posterity merely as the inventor of the Goldpepper Bridge and the Goldpepper Crown, and perfector of the Semi-Rectractable Clasp which bears his name.

The Certificate

The winter sunrise was still two hours away when Dr.
Roger Freeman came to stand in front of the great door.
By good fortune—incredibly good fortune—he had not
been questioned in his furtive progress from the dormitory. If he had been stopped, or if his answer had
been either disbelieved or judged inadequate, he might
have been sent back to the dorm for punishment. The
punishment would have been over, of course, in time for
him to go to work at ten in the morning, but a man
could suffer through several thousand eternities of Hell
in those few hours. And no more than a low muffled
groaning and a subdued convulsive movement of the
body to show what was going on. You were able to
sleep through it—if it was happening to someone else.

The great door was set well in from the street, and
the cutting edge of the wind was broken by it.

Freeman was grateful for that. It was two years ago
that he'd applied for a new overcoat, and the one he
still had was ragged even then. Perhaps—if this was not
to be his year for escape—in another year he would get

the coat. He crowded into a corner and tried not to think of the cold.

After a little while another man joined him, then another, then a woman, then a couple. By sunrise there was a long line. They were all willing to risk it, risk punishment for being out before work, or for being late to work. Some merely wanted clothes. Some wanted permission to visit relatives in another locale. You could wait years for either. Or, you could wait years and not get either. And some, like Freeman, hoped against hope for a chance to escape.

Dr. Freeman stared at the door. The design was as intricate as it was incomprehensible. No doubt it made sense to the Hedderans. If you could understand it you might gain some understanding of the nature of their distant home. If you cared. It was fifty years since they had arrived, and men still knew almost nothing about them.

They were here. They would never go away. That was enough.

The man behind Dr. Freeman collapsed. No one paid any attention to him. After a moment there was a high, brief humming. The man twitched, opened his eyes. He got to his feet.

And then the door opened.

"Proceed in the order," the voice directed—a thick, flat Hedderan voice; harsh, yet glutinous. No one tried to push ahead, the lesson had been too well learned. Dr. Freeman got on the third escalator, rode down two levels. There had been a time when you rode up—but that was before the Hedderans came. They didn't like tall buildings—at least it seemed so. They'd never explained—that, or anything else. What they did not like they simply destroyed.

Dr. Freeman looked behind him as he approached the office. There must have been at least a dozen people behind him. They looked at him wolfishly. So few certificates were granted, and he was first in line. He looked away. He'd stayed awake all night in order to *be* the first. No one had the right to resent him. And the next man in line was young. What did he expect . . . ?

The door opened, the voice said, *"Proceed one at a single time."* Fifty years, and the Hedderans still hadn't mastered the language. They didn't have to, of course. Roger Freeman entered the office, took the application form from the slot in the wall-machine found in every office, sat down at the table. When was the last time he had sat in a chair? No matter.

The form was in Hedderan, of course. The voice said, *"Name."* The voice said, *"Number."*

He wrote it down, Roger Freeman . . . 655-673-60-60-2. Idly he glanced at the cluster of Hedderan characters. If one could take the application form away, with Hedderan questions and English answers, perhaps—if there was time—a key could be found for translating. But it was impossible to take it away. If you spoiled it, you were out. You could apply only once a year. And if you *did* find out how to read their language, what then? Freeman's brother Bob had talked of rebellion—but that was years ago . . . and he didn't like to think what had happened to Bob. And besides, he hadn't *time*—he had to be at work by ten.

From ten in the morning until ten at night (the Hedderans had their own ways of reckoning time) he worked at a machine, pulling hard on levers. Some he had to bend down to reach, some he had to mount steps to reach. Up and down, up and down. He didn't know what the machine did, or even how it worked. And he no longer cared. He no longer cared about anything—except a new overcoat (or, at least, a newer one, not worn so thin), and his chances of escape.

Age. Occupation. Previous Occupation. Previous to the arrival of the Hedderans, that was. Fifty years ago. He had been a physician. An obsolete skill. Inside of every man nowadays there was a piece of . . . something . . . presumably it communicated with a machine somewhere deep in the Hedderan quarters. If you broke a bone or bled or even if you just fainted (as the young man behind him in line had), you were set right almost in the second. No one was ill for long—even worn-out organs were regenerated. Too few men had been left alive and the Hedderans needed those who were left too much to let them sicken or die.

At last the long form was filled out. The harsh voice said, *"Now at once to Office Ten, Level Four."*

Dr. Freeman hastily obeyed. When they said "at once," they meant just that. The punishment might come like a single whiplash—or it might go on and on. You never knew. Maybe the Hedderans knew. But they never told. The man next behind the outer door scuttled in as Freeman left. The others waited. Not more than three could expect to be processed before it would be time to return to work.

Office Ten, Level Four, asked him the same questions, but in a different order. He was then directed to Office Five, Level Seventeen. Here his two forms were fed into a machine, returned with markings stamped on them in Hedderan.

"Office Eight, Level Two," the voice said. There, he fed his applications into the slot. After a moment they came back—unmarked.

"Name Roger Freeman. Number 655-673-60-60-2. You

*have a single time application outstanding. Unpermitted
two. You will cancel this one. Or you will cancel that
one.*"

Frantically he searched his mind. What application did
he have outstanding? When was this rule made? The
overcoat! If he went ahead with this new application
and it was refused, he'd have to wait till next year to
reinstate the one for the coat. And then more years of
waiting . . . It was cold, the dormitory was ill-heated,
he had no blanket. His present coat was very worn.
Services for humans were minimal.

But he *had* to proceed with this new application. He
was first in line . . .

"*Speak*," the thick, flat voice directed. "*Answer. Speak.
Now.*"

Gobbling his words in haste, Freeman said, "I cancel
the one outstanding."

"*Insert forms.*"

He did. Waited.

"*Proceed to Office Ten, Level Four.*"

That was the second place he'd been to. A mistake?
No matter, he had to go. Once again he entered. And
waited.

A grunting noise caught his eye. He looked up, startled,
cowered. A Hedderan, his baffle-screen turned off, was
gazing at him. The blank, gray, faceted eyes in the
huge head, and the body, like a deformed foetus . . .
then the baffle-screen went on again. Freeman shuddered. One rarely saw them. It had been years.

A piece of paper slid from the machine. He took it
up, waiting for the command to proceed—where? Unless
it could be accomplished before ten, there was no
chance of escape for him this year. None whatever. He
stared dully at the strange characters. The cold, indif-

ferent voice said, "*Name Roger Freeman. Number 655-673-60-60-2. Declared surplus. Application for death certificate is granted. Proceed for certificate to Office One, Level Five. At once.*"

Tears rolled down Dr. Freeman's cheeks. "At last," he sobbed, joyfully. "At last . . ."

And then he hastily left. He had achieved his escape after all—but only if he got there before ten o'clock.

Ogre in the Vly

When the menace of Dr. Ludwig Sanzmann first arose, like a cloud no bigger than a man's hand, Dr. Fred B. Turbyfil, at twenty-seven, had been the youngest museum director in the country; and now at thirty-five he was still one of the youngest. Moreover, he had a confident, if precarious, hold on greater glories to come. High on the list of benefactors and patrons, Mr. Winfield Scott H. Godbody was an almost-dead (in more ways than one) certainly to will most of his substance to what would then become the Godbody Museum of Natural History: Dr. Fred B. Turbyfil, Director. The salary would be splendid, the expense account lavish and tax-free, and the Director would have ample time to finish his great work, at present entitled *Man Before the Dawn*—recondite, yet eminently readable. There were already seventeen chapters devoted to the Mousterian, or Neanderthal, Era alone. (It would be certain to sell forever to schools and libraries: a big book, firm in the grasp, profusely illustrated and done in so captivating a style that even a high school senior, picking it up unwarily in search of nudes, would be unable to extricate himself for hours.)

Mr. Godbody was a skeptic of the old-fashioned sort. "Where did Cain get his wife?" was a favorite cackle, accompanied by a nudge of his bony elbow. "Found any feathers from angels' wings yet?" was another.

He had pioneered in supplying cotton prints to flour millers for sacking. The brand name washed out, the figured cloth was then used for underwear and childrens' dresses by the thrifty farmers. This had made him a wealthy man, and increased his devotion to Science—the Science which had destroyed the cosmogony of the M.E. Church, South, and invented washable ink.

There was, at the moment, a minor hitch. Old Mr. Godbody affected to be shaken by the recent revelation of scandal in the anthropological hierarchy. From this respectable group, whose likenesses were known to every school child, long since having replaced Major and Minor Prophets alike in prestige and esteem, from this jolly little club—judgment falling like a bolt of thunder—the Piltdown Man had been expelled for cheating at cards. If Piltdown Man was a fake, he demanded querulously, why not all the rest? Java Man, Peiping Man, Austra-lopithecus tranvalensis—all bone-scraps, plaster of Paris, and wishful thinking? In vain, Turbyfil assured him that competent scholars had been leery of H. Piltdown for years; ugly old Mr. Godbody testily replied, "Then why didn't you say so?" Having lost one faith in his youth, the textile print prince was reluctant to lose another in his old age. But Dr. Turbyfil trusted his patron's doubt was only a passing phase. His chief anxiety, a well-modulated one, was whether Mr. Godbody's health would carry him over the few weeks or months necessary to get past this crochet.

In sum, Dr. Turbyfil was about to reap the rewards of virtue and honest toil, and when he reflected on this (as he often did) it amused him to sing—a trifle off-key —a song from his childhood, called "Bringing in the Sheaves." Prior to his coming to Holden, the museum —an architectural gem of the purest late Chester A. Arthur—had been headed by a senile, though deserving, Democrat, who had been washed into office on the high tide of the Free Silver movement. *And* the museum itself! Dr. Turbyfil found that every worthless collection of unsalable junk in the state made its way thither. Postage stamps of the sort sold by the pound on Nassau Street, stuffed and moldering opossums, tinted photographs of wall-eyed pioneers, hand-painted "china," unclassified arrowheads by the gross, buttons from Confederate uniforms, legislative gavels, mounted fish, geological "specimens" collected by people with no faintest knowledge of geology, tomahawks—oh, there was no end to the stuff.

That is, there had been no end to the stuff until the appointment of Dr. Fred B. Turbyfil . . . the trash still continued to come in, of course: there was no tactful way of stopping that. There were still many people to whom it seemed, when Uncle Tatum died, that the natural thing to do with Uncle Tatum's "collection" was to ship it to the Holden Museum. Dr. Turbyfil had developed his own technique of handling such shipments. He had them arranged—at night—in as many showcases as might be needed, prominently labeled with the donors' names; then he had the works photographed. To the contributory family, a gracious letter of thanks. To their local newspaper, a copy of the letter. To both family and paper, a Manila envelope of glossy prints. And then, for Uncle Tatum's musty nonsense, tomahawks and all, the blessed oblivion of the cellars. ("We are re-cataloguing," Dr. T. explained to the few inquirers.)

(*But you couldn't put Dr. Sanzmann in the cellar, could you?*)

The letters of thanks were worded in phrases as un-changing as a Buddhist litany. They extolled the career of the dead pioneer, gave proper credit to the sense of public interest displayed by his heirs, and hoped that their concern for the Important Work of the Holden Museum would be shared by others. The liturgical re-sponse was seldom wanting, and took the form of a check, the amount of which was, as Dr. Turbyfil had lightly pointed out, Deductable From Income Tax. *Om mani padme hum!*

Ah, that was a day when they opened the Hall of Practical Science! The governor, the senior U.S. senator, university presidents, hillbilly singers, and other public figures—scores of them. There was a real oil pump that pumped real oil, and a genuine cotton gin that ginned genuine cotton. It was the machines which set the tone for the exhibits, but Dr. Turbyfil was proudest of the huge photographic montages, mounted to give a three-dimensional effect. There was one of Mr. Opie Slawson (Slawson Oil and Natural Gas) pointing to the oil pool on the cross section (in natural color) of a typical oilif-erous area. There was another of Mr. Purvie Smith (P.S. Cotton and P.S. Food Products) watching his prize steers nuzzle cottonseed cake while replicas of the lean kine of Egypt stared hungrily at a clump of grass. There were others. And how the checks had come in! And continued to come!

(*But Doktor Philosoph. Ludwig Sanzmann was com-ing, too.*)

Months of preparation had gone into what was, after

all, really just a prestige exhibit—the display of Bouche
Perce Indian life before the Coming of the White Man.
A huge semi-circular backdrop gave the illusion of distance. Buffalo grazed conveniently not too far away,
and wild horses galloped along a hill crest. The primitive
Bouche Perces ground corn, played games, scraped
hides, wove weavings, put on war paint, rocked papooses,
and received the non-socialized ministrations of the
tribal medicine man. There were authentic wickiups,
simulated campfires, and a bona fide buffalo skull.

The Bouche Perces (who were "Oil Indians") drove
up in their Packards from miles around, and received
such a boost in tribal pride that they shortly afterward
filed suit for thirty million dollars against the Federal
Government. (They were finally awarded a judgment of
four million, most of which the Government deducted
to cover the expense of itself in allowing the Bouche
Perces to be swindled, cheated, and starved for the three
generations preceding the discovery of oil.) The Tribal
Council voted to make the museum the custodian of its
ceremonial regalia, and Dr. Turbyfil received several
honorary degrees and was made a member of learned
societies. The only opposition to his efforts on behalf of
American Indian culture came from the oldest (and
only surviving pure-blood) Bouche Perce. Her name was
Aunt Sally Weatherall, she was a prominent member of
the Baptist Ladies Auxiliary, and she steadfastly refused
his offer to be photographed with her in front of all them
Heathen Reliets and Nekked Women. She also added that
if her old granddaddy had ever caught any Bouche Perce
a-weaving *Navaho* blankets like that huzzy in the pitcher,
he'd of slit her wizzand.

The trouble was that Aunt Sally Weatherall *wouldn't*
come, and Dr. Sanzmann *would*. Any minute now.

Dr. Turbyfil had been expecting this visit for years. Dr. Sanzmann had mentioned it at every meeting. Sometimes his tones were bright and arch, sometimes they were gloomy and foreboding, and sometimes they were flat and brusque.

The two men had come to Holden within a few months of one another, Dr. Turbyfil from his two-year stay at the Museum of Natural Philosophy in Boston, and Professor Sanzmann from a meager living translating in New York, whither he had come as an exile from his native country. Sanzmann was politically quite pure, with no taint of either far right or near left; was, in fact, a Goethe scholar—and what can be purer than a Goethe scholar? He had a post at the local denominational university: Professor of Germanic *and* Oriental Languages, neatly skipping the questionable Slavs. Dr. Turbyfil was not an ungenerous man, and he was quite content to see Professor Sanzmann enjoy the full measure of linguistic success.

But Dr. Philosoph. Ludwig Sanzmann was also an amateur anthropologist, paleontologist, and general antiquarian: and this was enough to chill the blood of any museum director or even curator. Such amateurs are occupational hazards. They bring one smelly cow bone, and do it with a proud air of expectancy, fully anticipating the pronouncement of a new species of megatherium or brontosaurus. Although Dr. Sanzmann had not—so far—done *that,* he often put Turbyfil in mind of the verse,

"A little learning is a dangerous thing;
Drink deeply or touch not the Whozis Spring."

Ah, well, better to have it over with and done. It would be necessary to take a firm line, and then—

finished! No more hints of precious secrets, world-shaking discoveries, carefully guarded treasures, and so on.

When the Professor arrived, Dr. Turbyfil ran his left hand rapidly across his waving brown hair—still thick, praise be!—smiled his famous warm and boyish smile, held his right hand out in welcome. But with horror he saw that Sanzmann had a cardboard carton with him. The worst! Oh, the things one has to put up with . . . ! If not Mr. Godbody, then Professor—

"My dear Dr. Turbyfil! I have looked forward to this our meeting for so long! I cannot tell you—" But, of course, he would. He shook the proffered hand, sat down, held the carton as if it contained wedding cake, took out a handkerchief, wiped his rosy face, and panted. Then he began to speak.

"Dr. Turbyfil!" The name assumed the qualities of an indictment. "What is that which they used always to tell us? Urmensch—Primal Man, that is—he was a stunted little cre-a-ture, like a chimpanzee with a molybdenum deficiency, and he—which is to say, *we*—grew larger and bigger and more so, until, with the help of the actuarial tables of the insurance companies, we have our present great size attained and life expectancy. And we, pres-u-mably, will greater grow yet.

"*But!*" (Dr. Turbyfil quivered.) "What then comes to pass? An anthropologist goes into an Apotheke—a druck-store, yes?—in Peiping—oh, a bea-u-tiful city, I have been there, I love it with all my heart!—he goes into a native Chinese pharmacy, and there what is it that he finds? He finds—amongst the dried dragon bones, powdered bats, tigers' gall, rhinoceros horn, and pickled serpents—two human-like gigantic molar teeths. And then, behold, for this is wonderful! The whole picture changes!"

Oh my, oh my! thought Dr. Turbyfil.

"Now Primal Man becomes huge, tremendous, like the Sons of Anak in the First Moses-Book. We must now posit for him ancestors like the great apes of your Edgar Burroughs-Rice. And how it is that we, his children, have shrunken! Pit-i-ful! Instead of the pigs becoming elephants, the elephants are become pigs!" Dr. Sanzmann clicked his tongue.

"But that is nothing! Nothing at all: Wherefore have I come to you now? To make known to you a something that is so much more startling. I must begin earlier than our own times. Charles the Fifth!"

Dr. Turbyfil quavered. "I beg your pardon?"

"Charles the Fifth of Hapsburg. In 1555 Charles the Emperor resigns, no, retires? Abdicates. His brother Ferdinand succeeds him as sovereign of the Hapsburg dominions, and Charles retreats himself to a monastery.

"'With age, with cares, with maladies oppres't,

"'He seeks the refuge of monastic rest—'"

"Ahhh, Professor *Sanz*mann," Dr. Turbyfil began, stopped, blinked.

"Yes—yes: I *di*-gress. Well. Charles and Ferdinand. A medallion is struck, Charles, one side—Ferdinand the other. And the date, 1555. Here is the medallion." Dr. Sanzmann reached into an inner pocket and pulled out a flat little box, such as jewelers use. He opened it.

Inside lay a blackened disk about the size of a silver dollar, and a piece of paper with two rubbings—the profiles of two men, Latin mottoes, and the date: 1555. Completely at sea, and feeling more and more sorry for himself, Dr. Turbyfil looked at his rosy-faced and gray-haired caller; made a small, bewildered gesture.

"Soon, soon, you will understand everything. Nineteen thirty. My vacations—I am still in Chair-many—I spend at Maldenhausen, a little rural hamlet in a walley. Then things are quiet. Ah, these Chairman walleys! So green, remote, enchanting, full of mysteries! I drink beer and wine, I smoke my pipe, and go on long walks in the countryside. And—since I am a scholar, and ever the dog returns to his womit—I spend also some time in the willage archives . . . Many interesting things . . . A child named Simon . . .

"In 1555 a child named Simon is stolen by an ogre."

Dr. Turbyfil pressed a fist to his forehead and moaned faintly. "Is—*what?*" he said, fretfully.

"Please. You see the hole in the medallion? The child Simon wore it about his neck on a thong. They were very reverend, these peasant people. An Imperial medallion, one wears it on one's bosom. A photostatic copy of the testimony." Professor Sanzmann opened the box, removed papers. Photostatic copies, indeed, were among them, but the language was a monkish Latin, and in Gothic lettering. Dr. Turbyfil felt his eyes begin to hurt him, closed them. Professor Sanzmann, dreadful man, spoke on. There were two witnesses, an old man of the name Sigismund, a boy called Lothar. It was winter. It was snow. The child Simon runs with his dog down the field. He shouts. He is afraid. Out of the snow behind him the ogre comes. He is just as they always knew ogres to be: huge, hairy, crooked, clad in skins, carrying a cudgel. Terrible.

"Lothar runs for help. The old man cannot run, so he stays. And prays. The ogre seizes up the child Simon and runs away with him, back into the fields, toward the hills, until the snow hides them.

"The people are aroused, they are fearful, but not surprised. This happens. There are wolves, there are bears, there are ogres. Such are the hazards of living on the remote farms."

Dr. Turbyfil shivered. A chill crept into his flesh. He rubbed his fingers to warm them. "Folklore," he croaked. "Old wives' tales."

Dr. Sanzmann waved his hands, then placed them on the photostats. "This is not the Brothers Grimm," he said. "These are contemporary accounts with eyewitnesses. I continue. The people go out in the storm, with dogs and pikes and even a few matchlocks; and since they huddle fearingly together and the snow has hid all footmarks, it is not a surprise that they do not find the child or the ogre's spoor. The dog, yes—but he is quite dead. Crushed. One tremendous blow. The next day they search, and then the next, and then no more. Perhaps in the spring they will find some bones for Christian burial . . .

"The child had been warned that if he went too far from home he would be stolen by an ogre. He *did* go too far from home, and he *was* stolen by an ogre. So. Fifteen sixty."

Dr. Turbyfil ventured a small smile. "The child has been dead for five years." He felt better now that he knew what was in the carton. He visualized the card which would never, certainly *never*, be typed! *"Bones of child devoured by ogre in 1555. Gift of Prof. Ludwig Sanzmann, Dr. Phil."*

The Goethe scholar swept on. "In 1560 the child Simon," he said, "is discovered trying to pilfer fowls from a farmyard in the nexten walley. He is naked, filthy, long-haired, lousy. He growls and cannot speak coherent speech. He fights. It is very sad."

The museum director agreed that it was very sad. (Then what *was* in the carton?)

"Child Simon is tied, he is delivered up to his parents, who must lock him in a room to keep him from escaping. Gradually he learns to speak again. And then comes to see him the Burgomeister, and the notary, and the priest, and the Baron, and I should imagine half the people of the district, and they ask him to tell his story, speaking ever the truth.

"The ogre (he says) carried him away very distantly and high up, to his cave, and there in his cave is his wife the ogress, and a small ogre, who is their child. At first Simon fears they will consume him, but no. He is brought to be a companion to the ogre child, who is ill. And children are adaptive, very adaptive. Simon plays with the ogre child, and the ogre brings back sheep and wenison and other foods. At first it is hard for Simon to eat the raw meat, so the ogress chews it soft for him—"

"Please!" Dr. Turbyfil held up a protesting hand, but Professor Sanzmann neither saw nor heard him. With gleaming eyes gazing into the distance he went on.

"It comes the spring. The ogre family sports in the forest, and Simon with him. Then comes again the autumn and winter and at last the ogre child dies. It is sad. The parents cannot believe it. They moan to him. They rock him in their arms. No use. They bury him finally beneath the cave floor. *Now* you will ask," he informed the glassy-eyed Turbyfil, "do they smear the body with red ocher as a symbol of life, of blood and flesh, as our scientists say? No. And why not? Because he is already smeared. All of them. All the time. They like it so. It is not early religion, it is early cosmetic, only."

He sighed. Dr. Turbyfil echoed it.

"And so, swiftly pass the years," Professor Sanzmann patted his hand on the empty air to indicate the passing years. "The old ogre is killed by a she-bear and then the ogress will not eat. She whimpers and clasps Simon to her, and presently she grows cold and is dead. He is alone. The rest we know. Simon grows up, marries, has children, dies. But there are no more ogres.

"Not ever.

"Naturally, I am fascinated. I ask the peasants, where is there a cave called the Cave of the Ogres? They look at me with slanting glances, but will not answer. I am patient. I come back each summer. Nineteen thirty-one. Nineteen thirty-two. Nineteen thirty-three. Everyone knows me. I give small presents to the children. By myself I wander in the hills and search for caves. Nineteen thirty-four. There is a cow-tending child in the high pastures. We are friends. I speak of a cave near there. This, I say, is called Cave of the Ogres. The child laughs. No, no, he says, for that is another cave: it is located thus and so.

"And I find it where he says. But I am circumspect. I wait another year. Then I come and I make my private excavations. And—I—find—this."

He threw open the carton and unwrapped from many layers of cotton wool something brown and bony, and he set it in front of Dr. Turbyfil.

"There was a fairly complete skeleton, but I took just the skull and jawbone. You recognize it at once, of course. And with it I found, as I expected, the medallion of Charles and Ferdinand. Simon had allowed them to bury it with the ogre child because he had been fond of it. It is all written in the photostatic paper copies . . . In 1936 the Nazis—"

Dr. Turbyfil stared at the skull. "No, no, no, no," he whispered. It was not a very large skull. "No, no, no," he whispered, staring at the receding forehead and massive chinless jaw, the bulging eye ridges.

"So, tell me now, sir museum director: Is this not a find more remarkable than big teeths in a Peiping herb shop?" His eyes seemed very young, and very bright.

Dr. Turbyfil thought rapidly. It needed just something like this to set the Sunday supplements and Mr. Godbody ablaze and ruin forever both his reputation and that of the Holden Museum. Years and years of work—the seventeen chapters on the Mousterian Era alone in *Man Before the Dawn*—the bequest from old Mr. Godbody—

Then the thought sprang fully-formed in his mind: Where there had been *one* skeleton, there must be others, unspoiled by absurd sixteenth-century paraphernalia—which had no business being there, anyway. He arose, placed a hand on Professor Sanzmann's shoulder.

"My friend," he said, in warm, golden, dulcet tones. "My friend, it will take some time before the Sanzmann Expedition of the Holden Museum will be ready to start. While you make the necessary personal preparations to lead us to the site of your truly astounding discovery, please oblige me by saying nothing about this to our—alas—unscholarly and often sensational press. Eh?"

Dr. Sanzmann's rosy face broke into a thousand wrinkles and tears of joy and gratitude rolled down his cheeks. Dr. Turbyfil generously pretended not to see.

"Imagine what a revolution this will produce," he said, as if he were thinking aloud. "Instead of being tidily extinct for fifty thousand years, our poor cousins survived into modern times. Fantastic! Our whole timetable will have to be rewritten . . ." His voice died away. His eyes focused on Professor Sanzmann, nodding his head, sniffling happily, as he tied up his package.

"Incidentally, my dear Professor," he said: "before you leave I must show you some interesting potsherds that were dug up not a mile from here. You will be fascinated.

Aztec influences! This way . . . mind the stairs. I am afraid our cellar is not very well arranged at present; we have been recataloguing . . . this fascinating collection formerly belonged to a pioneer figure, the late Mr. Tatum Tompkins."

Behind a small mountain of packing cases, Dr. Turbyfil dealt Professor Sanzmann a swift blow on the temple with one of Uncle Tatum's tomahawks. The sinister Continental scholar fell without a sound, his rosy lips opened upon an unuttered aspirate. Dr. Turbyfil made shift to bury him in the farthest corner of the cellar, and to pile upon his grave such a pyramid of uncatalogued horrors as need not, God and Godbody willing, be disturbed for several centuries.

Dusting his hands, and whistling—a trifle off-key—the hymn called "Bringing in the Sheaves," Dr. Turbyfil returned to the office above stairs. There he opened an atlas, looking at large-scale maps of Germany. A village named Maldenhausen, in a valley . . . (Where there had been *one* skeleton, there must be others, unspoiled by absurd sixteenth-century paraphernalia—which had no business being there.) His fingers skipped joyfully along the map, and in his mind's eye he saw himself already in those valleys, with their lovely names: Friedenthal, Johannesthal, Hochsthal, Neanderthal, Waldenthal . . . beautiful valleys! Green, remote, enchanting . . . full of mysteries.

Après Nous

Doctor Boswell's time machine was actually four time machines, four devices looking like the work of an insane clockmaker. Arranged in a rectangle (or, to be just a shade more precise, a diamond pattern) and set to functioning, they produced the Boswell Effect.

It is by now a truism that only three people in the entire world ever fully understood the Boswell Effect. One of these was the laconic Professor Spencer Peabody of ULCS—whose abrupt departure for the Amazonian slopes of the Andes with a portable sawmill later created a furore in academic circles and was almost a nine days' wonder (the attention of the keen-eyed press was diverted on the eighth day by an ax murder of uncommon juiciness).

"As yet," Dr. Boswell repeated to Professor Peabody just prior to the first test of the machines, "I have no way of knowing how long a period of time is represented by each graduation of the dial. It is my hope that the control animals will return with specimens of organic matter—either caught in their pelts, or in process of ingestion—and that, by an entirely novel use of the radio-

carbon process, we shall learn how far into the future
each has traveled."

The Boswell Effect, for reasons as yet only dimly
guessed at, could not be used to visit the past.

"Quite," said Professor Peabody.

Dr. Boswell lifted the guinea pig out of its cage and
set it down in the center of the diamond. He adjusted
the dial to one mark, threw the switch. Then they had
lunch. Then Dr. Boswell reversed the switch. But nothing
happened. With no more than a philosophical shrug the
two men selected a hamster and repeated the experiment,
setting the dial ahead two marks. The result was again
negative.

"After supper we shall try another hamster, at the next
mark," said Dr. Boswell; "and we will give this one even
more time."

"Quite," said Professor Peabody. They had supper, and
the second hamster was presently sent into the future.
Several hours later Dr. Boswell for the third time reversed the switch. Abruptly, with a twitch and a shimmer,
the hamster came.

Its once sleek pelt was rough and damp and matted.
Its eyes were no longer bright, but dull. It panted for air
with feeble movements. But—held firmly in its teeth was
a piece of organic matter.

"I am not a botanist," said Dr. Boswell, with his customary modesty, "but I think—I rather incline to think—
isn't that an olive leaf?"

"Quite," said Professor Peabody.

Climacteric

They had driven up, just the two of them, to a place
in the mountains he had spoken of—store, garage, hotel,
all in one—it was a rare day, a vintage day, with no one
to bother them while they ate lunch and shared a bottle
of wine. She spoke most; the things she said were silly,
really, but she was young and she was lovely and this
lent a shimmer of beauty to her words.

His eyes fed upon her—the golden corona of her hair,
the green topazes of her eyes, exquisitely fresh skin,
creamy column of neck, her bosom (O twin orbs of sweet
delight!)—

"But never mind that," she said, ceasing what she had
been saying. "I want to forget all that. You: What were
you like as a boy? What did you dream of?"

He smiled. "Of a million beautiful girls—all like you,"
he added, as she made a pretty pout with her red little
mouth—"and how I would rescue them from a hideous
dragon, piercing through its ugly scales with my lance,"
he said, "while its filthy claws scrabbled on the rocks in
a death agony . . . And the girl and I lived happily ever
after, amid chaste kisses, nothing more."

She smiled, touched him. "Lovely," she said. "But— chaste kisses? Now, I used to dream—but never mind. It's funny how our dreams change, and yet, not so much, isn't it?" They looked swiftly about, saw nothing but a distant bird, speck-small in the sky; then they kissed.

Very soon afterward, they drove up a side road to the end, then climbed a path. "You're quite sure no one can see us here?" she asked.

"Quite sure," he said. He stepped back. There was a noise of great rushing, then a short scream, then—other noises. After a while he drew nearer and ran his hands lovingly over the sparkling and iridescent scales. The beautiful creature hissed appreciatively, and continued to clean its gorgeous and glittering claws with its shining black bifurcated tongue.

Yo-Ho, and Up

It was past two, stars sharp and shining in the cold sky, but Andy couldn't wait till morning. He had seen the light in Hank's backyard, and as soon as he had parked the car, that's where he went. Hank was crouched, rasping a hinge with a file. His face was frowning, intent.

"Greetings, Earthman," said Andy. One side of Hank's face quirked, but he kept on at his job. The latest fad; all the 12 to 16 set was working overtime at it. But Andy was past that age. "Hey!" he yipped, eagerly. "Aren't you going to *ask* me—?"

Hank looked puzzled. Then his face changed. "Oh," he said. "Yeah. You and Bitsy-Lee . . . Well—how did you make out?"

Andy told him, in great detail, his voice gloating. "When you're a little bit older," he said, at last, "maybe I can fix you up. She's got this friend, see—" Hank nodded slowly, the file drooping in his hand, as if it were very heavy. Far-off, a light toiled through the sky, was gone.

"And her *father!*" Andy triumphed. "—Almost didn't let us out of the house! I thought I'd—" Another light: meteor. "—or turn *green!* 'Never before have our youths matured so early,' he was yacking, '—voices changing

sooner, and so on,' he said; 'and never has it taken so
long for them to fill their own niches in society.' Bla-bla-
bla. 'Military service, college, post-graduate, high cost of
living, anxieties and tensions—' Oh, well, hell with *him*.
She—"

Hank put the file in the tool-box. "No, go on," he said.
"What else did he—"

"*Pol*tergeists, is what he was talking about! 'Wherever
there's a poltergeist, there's a child emerging from pu-
berty.' Hoo, boy! 'Raw, fresh, sexual energy is being produced earlier, narrowed and channelized in its effect by
the circumstances of our society—' And so on. 'Like a
blast furnace!' the old man said. —Boy, we did some blast-
ing ourselves, Bitsy-Lee and me," he muttered. "We—"

He stopped. The tool-box moved across the yard all
by itself. His eyes, wild, met Hank's. "You can do it,"
the kid said. "Try. *Try!*" Something stirred in Andy: suddenly he knew he could, had known for some time. *It
was easy!* Then he groaned. No use. The night and its
new-found pleasures had drained him forever. The night
—now full of shooting-stars . . . but meteors went *down*,
not *up!*

The tool-box fell with a crash. "Don't strain your milk,
Dad," Hank said, mockingly. There was a roar and a
burst of light from not far away. Another—and another.
"We're off," Hank said. "Boys and girls together." He
waved his hand widely. "*This*—it's all yours. But don't
try to come after us. Where we're going, we don't want—"
His last words were drowned out as he stepped into his
home-made "space-ship" and slammed the door. An instant later Andy lay stunned on his back. *He's only a
kid!* he thought, wildly; *he never even made out!* But the
stars burned and beckoned even after the other lights had
vanished.

The Sixty-Third Street Station

Arthur Hughey would rather have gotten on one of them new IRT trains, but it would have been silly to wait in the station for another just because the one which pulled in was of the old type. It was about time, he thought, that the Transit Authority gave the IRT rider some consideration: Everything lavished on the IND or the BMT, and the third system left forlorn.

But, sitting in the old coach, he knew that he really preferred it. He did not really like new things, changed things. And he knew that eventually he would wait in the stations—wait and pass up the new trains and get in one of the old coaches—as long as there were old coaches. This was sure to make him late, and he hated being late, hated any breaks in familiar schedules. I am a creature of habit, he thought, with some satisfaction.

Then it hit him. For a moment he'd forgotten. He wouldn't be riding the IRT much longer, anyway. He was going to make a mighty big change, he was going to break the whole pattern of his life. And he hadn't yet told his sister. He felt a little sick.

The train went roaring down slopes and tearing around

curves. Automatically, Arthur reached for a newspaper which wasn't there. How many years had he read the *Sun* in the subway (a joke which never lost savor for him) on the way home? Now there was no more *Sun* and he was unable to accustom himself to the fact. I am a creature of habit.

That was why he always got in the fifth coach: the end coaches were unsafe. Suppose the train ran into another? Or another ran into it from the other end?

"You can set the clock by Arthur," his sister Fanny said. Often. Well, she's going to have to set it by someone else. He looked around the car. The woman in the ugly hat was in her corner, chewing gum and reading the *News*. She never missed the demise of the *Sun*. Did someone set a clock by her? Because she'd been in the fifth coach, too, almost every night for a long time.

"Will your sister miss you much?" Anna had asked him. Anna. There was a nice, old-fashioned sound about that name. Not Anne: Anna. *Where thou, great Anna, whom three realms obey*—well. Would Fanny miss him? He had simply shrugged, and Anna said, "Oh, well, she'll get used to it. She can visit us and we'll visit her—real often . . . When am I going to meet her, Arthur?"

When indeed? When was the last time Fanny had visited anyone? Or anyone visited them? He didn't recall the last visitor they'd had, but the last visit they had paid was to old Mrs. Whittier in the Methodist Home in Riverdale, shortly before she died. Since then they had spent every evening at home, reading, listening to the radio—Fanny hadn't wanted a TV—"Where would we put it, Arthur?" "We could put the sideboard in storage (he hadn't dared suggest selling it or giving it away)." "*Arthur! Mother's sideboard?*"—listening to the radio, reading, he working on his stamp collection, she doing her needlework, or knitting, for the church. They no longer attended on Sunday, but Fanny still sent in her work. Quiet evenings.

"Why forty-five isn't old!" And Anna really thought so. She owned her home in Queens. That was where they'd live. And what would Fanny do? Fanny would die. She had put so much of life away from her, it would be no effort to let go of what remained. Well, he'd think of that later. Thinking of it now made him feel sick. Ninety-Sixth Street Station. Then Seventy-Second Street. Then Sixty-Third Street. He smiled.

That was one of those little private jokes he shared with Anna. No, forty-five wasn't old. And Anna wasn't yet forty. They might have children, no reason why they shouldn't have children . . . A private little joke about the Sixty-Third Street Station. He wasn't sure she would believe him when he told her.

They had lunch at the Automat. The lunch which Fanny packed for him he gave to the elevator man. He couldn't throw it away. "Did you know there's an IRT station which isn't on the maps in the subways?" he asked.

"How do you *know?*" And she smiled and opened her eyes wide and was delighted.

"I *see* it. Sixty-Third Street. It must be a local stop. I take the express so we never stop there, just kind of slow up a little because it's at the top of a slope. But it isn't on the subway map."

So she would stop by his desk in the office where they worked and smile and ask, "What's new at Sixty-Third Street?" Or he would say, "I had a date with Mabel last night." That was the name he'd given to the woman in the ugly hat. He'd say, "We went with Legs and Shoulders to the penny arcade"—something like that. Anna and he got a lot of fun out of it.

The woman's name *had* to be Mabel. That was the kind of woman she was. And the two men he usually saw waiting on the platform at Sixty-Third Street—well, he just *knew* that they were called Legs and Shoulders: that padded-out jacket, those long, long limbs—they couldn't be called anything else.

The train came to Seventy-Second Street and again Arthur felt sick. What he was doing was right. A man should marry. It wasn't his fault that Fanny had built no life for herself. He shouldn't be expected to give his up— But he knew the arguments too well. He and Fanny had lived alone for twenty-five years. Since Mother died. Fanny would not believe him. He knew her. And when, finally she *did* believe him, what then? He felt cold and ill. And he knew that it was impossible. He couldn't do it. He gazed with anguish at the bleak subway station. There was a sign there among the advertisements, one of those Bible Society posters. *Now, therefore choose life, that ye may live.*

But he couldn't. He simply couldn't do it.

He must get off at the next stop and call Anna and tell her. There was nothing else. The train pulled out of Seventy-Second Street. Now that he had made up his mind, Arthur no longer felt ill. Just a little numb. He would get off at the next stop, call Anna. Not put it off for a minute.

The train went baying up the slope, slowed down at Sixty-Third Street, stopped. Arthur jumped to his feet. It had never stopped here before. The doors opened. Get out and call Anna. He stood, irresolute. The woman in the ugly hat looked up and caught his eye.

"Hurry," she said. "They'll only be here a minute. Hur-ry!"

"I can't give her up," Arthur found himself explaining, pleading.

"*Hur-ry!*" It was no use. He had to give her up.

He started out. Legs and Shoulders grinned at him, grinned broadly.

"Look who's here!" said Legs.

"Well, at last!" said Shoulders.

The train started with a click and a clatter. The woman in the ugly hat began a scream that went on and on and on. The train ground to a halt. She stopped screaming. She put a stick of gum in her mouth, turned a page in her newspaper, and began to read.

"If they'd put a steering wheel or something on this thing," Legs said, "one man could do it alone."

"You always got a beef. Easy on the curve," said Shoulders. The lights were very bright.

"Well, I thought for a while here we weren't going to make our quota," Legs remarked. "Fifty-one, fifty-two."

"We *always* make our quota. Don't the Boss see to it? Sometimes," Shoulders pointed out, "it just takes a little longer; that's all. Fifty-eight—Hey. The beer still cold in fifty-nine?"

Legs sounded a bit hurt. "Fifty-nine is always reserved for beer," he said. "No matter *what* happens: no warm beer. Sixty-one—"

"Sixty-two. Sixty-Three. *Here* we are," said Shoulders, cheerfully. He pulled the long, deep drawer all the way out. "Every modern convenience," he said. "Got your end?"

"Got it," Legs said. "*Up* we go. Easy. Easy. That's right."

The units were well-designed; the stretcher was a perfect fit.

"Well . . . I guess . . ." Shoulders grunted a bit. "I guess we buy Mabel a new hat."

"Guess so," Legs answered. "Good old Mabel."

They gave the drawer a push and it rolled back in with a click and a clatter.

The House the Blakeneys Built

"Four people coming down the Forest Road, a hey," Old Big Mary said.

Young Red Tom understood her at once. "Not ours."

Things grew very quiet in the long kitchenroom. Old Whitey Bill shifted in his chairseat. "Those have's to be Runaway Little Bob's and that Thin Jinnie's," he said. "Help me up, some."

"No," Old Big Mary said. "They're not."

"Has to be." Old Whitey Bill shuffled up, leaning on his canestick. "Has to be. Whose elses could they be. Always said, me, she ran after him."

Young Whitey Bill put another chunk of burnwood on the burning. "Rowwer, rowwer," he muttered. Then everyone was talking at once, crowding up to the windowlooks. Then everybody stopped the talking. The big foodpots bubbled. Young Big Mary mumbletalked excitedly. Then her words came out clearsound.

"Look to here—look to here—I say, me, they aren't Blakeneys."

Old Little Mary, coming down from the spindleroom, called out, "People! People! Three and four of them down the Forest Road and I don't know them and, oh, they funnywalk!"

"Four strange people!"

"Not Blakeneys!"

"Stop sillytalking! Has to be! Who elses?"

"But not Blakeneys!"

"Not from The House, look to, look to! People—not from The House!"

"Runaway Bob and that Thin Jinnie?"

"No, can't be. No old ones."

"Children? Childrenchildren?"

All who hadn't been lookseeing before came now, all who were at The House, that is—running from the cowroom and the horseroom and dairyroom, ironroom, schoolroom, even from the sickroom.

"Four people! Not Blakeneys, some say!"

"Blakeneys or not Blakeneys, not from The House!"

Robert Hayakawa and his wife Shulamith came out of the forest, Ezra and Mikicho with them. "Well, as I said," Robert observed, in his slow careful way, "a road may end nowhere, going in one direction, but it's not likely it will end nowhere, going in the other."

Shulamith sighed. She was heavy with child. "Tilled fields. I'm glad of that. There was no sign of them anywhere else on the planet. This must be a new settlement. But we've been all over that—" She stopped abruptly, so did they all.

Ezra pointed. "A house—"

"It's more like a, well, what would you say?" Mikicho moved her mouth, groping for a word. "A . . . a *castle?* Robert?"

Very softly, Robert said, "It's not new, whatever it is. It is very much not new, don't you see, Shulamith. *What—?*"

She had given a little cry of alarm, or perhaps just surprise. All four turned to see what had surprised her. A man was running over the field towards them. He stopped, stumbling, as they all turned to him. Then he started again, a curious shambling walk. They could see his mouth moving after a while. He pointed to the four, waved his hand, waggled his head.

"Hey," they could hear him saying. "A hey, a hey. Hey. Look to. Mum. Mum mum mum. Oh, hey . . ."

He had a florid face, a round face that bulged over the eyes, and they were prominent and blue eyes. His nose was an eagle's nose, sharp and hooked, and his mouth was loose and trembling. "Oh, hey, you must be, mum, his name, what? And she run off to follow him? Longlong. Jinnie! Thin Jinnie! Childrenchildren, a hey?" Behind him in the field two animals paused before a plow, switching their tails.

"Michiko, look," said Ezra. "Those must be cows."

The man had stopped about ten feet away. He was dressed in loose, coarse cloth. Again he waggled his head. "Cows, no. Oh, no, mum mum, freemartins, elses. Not cows." Something occurred to him, almost staggering in its astonishment. "A hey, you won't know me! Won't know me!" He laughed. "Oh. What a thing. Strange Blakeneys. Old Red Tom, I say, me."

Gravely, they introduced themselves. He frowned, his slack mouth moving. "Don't know them name," he said, after a moment. "No, a mum. Make them up, like children, in the woods. Longlong. Oh, I, now! Runaway Little Bob. Yes, that name! Your fatherfather. Dead, a hey?"

Very politely, very wearily, feeling—now that he had stopped—the fatigue of the long, long walk, Robert Hayakawa said, "I'm afraid I don't know him. We are not, I think, who you seem to think we are . . . might we go on to the house, do you know?" His wife murmured her agreement, and leaned against him.

Old Red Tom, who had been gaping, seemed suddenly to catch at a word. "The House! A hey, yes. Go on to The House. Good now. Mum."

They started off, more slowly than before, and Old Red Tom, having unhitched his freemartins, followed behind, from time to time calling something unintelligible. "A funny fellow," said Ezra.

"He talks so *oddly,*" Mikicho said. And Shulamith said that all she wanted was to sit down. Then—

"Oh, look," she said. "*Look!*"

"They have all come to greet us," her husband observed.

And so they had.

Nothing like this event had ever occurred in the history of the Blakeneys. But they were not found wanting. They brought the strangers into The House, gave them the softest chairseats, nearest to the burning; gave them cookingmilk and cheesemeats and tatoplants. Fatigue descended on the newcomers in a rush; they ate and drank somewhat, then they sank back, silent.

But the people of the house were not silent, far from it. Most of them who had been away had now come back, they milled around, some gulping eats, others craning and staring, most talking and talking and talking—few of them mumbletalking, now that the initial excitement had ebbed a bit. To the newcomers, eyes now opening with effort, now closing, despite, the people of the house seemed like figures from one of those halls of mirrors they had read about in social histories: the same faces, clothes . . . but, ah, indeed, not the same dimensions. Everywhere—florid complexions, bulging blue eyes, protruding bones at the forehead, hooked thin noses, flabby mouths.

Blakeneys.

Thin Blakeneys, big Blakeneys, little Blakeneys, old ones, young ones, male and female. There seemed to be one standard model from which the others had been stretched or compressed, but it was difficult to conjecture what this exact standard was.

"Starside, then," Young Big Mary said—and said again and again, clearsound. "No elses live to Blakeneyworld. Starside, Starside, a hey, Starside. Same as Captains."

Young Whitey Bill pointed with a stick of burnwood at Shulamith. "Baby grows," he said. "Rower, rower. Baby soon."

With a great effort, Robert roused himself. "Yes. She's going to have a baby very soon. We will be glad of your help."

Old Whitey Bill came for another look to, hobbling on his canestick. "We descend," he said, putting his face very close to Robert's, "we descend from the Captains. Hasn't heard of them, you? Elses not heard? Funny. Funnyfunny. We descend, look to. From the Captains. Captain Tom Blakeney. And his wives. Captain Bill Blakeney. And his wives. Brothers, they. Jinnie, Mary, Captain Tom's wives. Other Mary, Captain Bob's wife. Had another wife, but we don't remember it, us, her name. They lived, look to. Starside. You, too? Mum, you? A hey, Starside?"

Robert nodded. "When?" he asked. "When did they come from Starside? The brothers."

Night had fallen, but no lights were lit. Only the dancing flames, steadily fed, of the burning, with chunks and chunks of fat and greasy burnwood, flickered and illuminated the great room. "Ah, when," said Old Red Tom, thrusting up to the chairseat. "When we children, old Blakeneys say, a hey, five hundredyear. Long-long."

Old Little Mary said, suddenly, "They funnywalk. They funnytalk. But, oh, they funnylook, too!"

"A baby. A baby. Grows a baby, soon."

And two or three little baby Blakeneys, like shrunken versions of their elders, gobbled and giggled and asked to see the Starside baby. The big ones laughed, told them, soon.

"Five hundred . . ." Hayakawa drowsed. He snapped awake. "The four of us," he said, "were heading in our boat for the Moons of Lor. Have you—no, I see, you never have. It's a short trip, really. But something happened to us, I don't know . . . how to explain it . . . we ran into something . . . something that wasn't there. A warp? A hole? That's silly, I know, but—it was as though we felt the boat *drop,* somehow. And then, after that, our instruments didn't work and we saw we had no celestial references . . . not a star we knew. What's that phrase, 'A new Heaven and a new Earth?' We were just able to reach her. Blakeneyworld, as you call it."

Sparks snapped and flew. Someone said, "Sleepytime." And then all the Blakeneys went away and then Hayakawa slept.

It was washtime when the four woke up, and all the Blakeneys around The House, big and little, were off scrubbing themselves and their clothes. "I guess that food on the table is for us," Ezra said. "I will assume it is for us. Say grace, Robert. I'm hungry."

Afterwards they got up and looked around. The room was big and the far end so dark, even with sunshine pouring in through the open shutters, that they could hardly make out the painting on the wall. The paint was peeling, anyway, and a crack like a flash of lightning ran through it; plaster or something of the sort had been slapped onto it, but this had mostly fallen out, its only lasting effect being to deface the painting further.

"Do you suppose that the two big figures could be the Captains?" Mikicho asked, for Robert had told them what Old Whitey Bill had said.

"I would guess so. They look grim and purposeful . . . When was the persecution of the polygamists, anybody know?"

Current social histories had little to say about that period, but the four finally agreed it had been during the Refinishing Era, and that this had been about six hundred years ago. "Could this house be that old?" Shulamith asked. "Parts of it, I suppose, could be. I'll tell you what I think, *I* think that those two Captains set out like ancient patriarchs with their wives and their families and their flocks and so on, heading for somewhere where they wouldn't be persecuted. And then they hit—well, whatever it was that *we* hit. And wound up here. Like us."

Mikicho said, in a small, small voice, "And perhaps it will be another six hundred years before anyone else comes here. Oh, we're here for good and forever. That's sure."

They walked on, silent and unsure, through endless corridors and endless rooms. Some were clean enough, others were clogged with dust and rubbish, some had fallen into ruin, some were being used for barns and stables, and in one was a warm forge.

"Well," Robert said at last, "we must make the best of it. We cannot change the configurations of the universe."

Following the sounds they presently heard brought them to the washroom, slippery, warm, steamy, noisy.

Once again they were surrounded by the antic Blakeney face and form in its many permutations. "Washtime, washtime!" their hosts shouted, showing them where to put their clothes, fingering the garments curiously, help- ing them to soap, explaining which of the pools were fed by hot springs, which by warm and cold, giving them towels, assisting Shulamith carefully.

"Your world house, you, a hey," began a be-soaped Blakeney to Ezra; "bigger than this? No."

Ezra agreed, "No."

"Your—Blakeneys? No. Mum, mum. Hey. Family? Smaller, a hey?"

"Oh, much smaller."

The Blakeney nodded. Then he offered to scrub Ezra's back if Ezra would scrub his.

The hours passed, and the days. There seemed no government, no rules, only ways and habits and prac- tices. Those who felt so inclined, worked. Those who didn't . . . didn't. No one suggested the newcomers do anything, no one prevented from doing anything. It was perhaps a week later that Robert and Ezra invited them- selves on a trip along the shore of the bay. Two healthy horses pulled a rickety wagon.

The driver's name was Young Little Bob. "Gots to fix a floorwalk," he said. "In the, a hey, in the sickroom. Needs boards. Lots at the riverwater."

The sun was warm. The House now and again van- ished behind trees or hills, now and again, as the road curved with the bay, came into view, looming over every- thing.

"We've got to find something for ourselves to *do*," Ezra said. "These people may be all one big happy fam- ily, they better be, the only family on the whole planet all this time. But if I spend any much more time with them I think I'll become as dippy as they are."

Robert said, deprecatingly, that the Blakeneys weren't *very* dippy. "Besides," he pointed out, "sooner or later our children are going to have to intermarry with them, and—"

"Our children can intermarry with each other—"

"Our grandchildren, then. I'm afraid we haven't the ancient skills necessary to be pioneers, otherwise we might go . . . just anywhere. There is, after all, lots of room. But in a few hundred years, perhaps less, our descendents would be just as inbred and, well, odd. This way, at least, there's a chance. Hybrid vigor, and all that."

They forded the river at a point just directly opposite The House. A thin plume of smoke rose from one of its great, gaunt chimneys. The wagon turned up an overgrown path which followed up the river. "Lots of boards," said Young Little Bob. "Mum mum mum."

There were lot of boards, just as he said, weathered a silver gray. They were piled under the roof of a great open shed. At the edge of it a huge wheel turned and turned in the water. It, like the roof, was made of some dull and unrusted metal. But only the wheel turned. The other machinery was dusty.

"Millstones," Ezra said. "And saws. Lathes. And . . . all sorts of things. Why do they—Bob? Young Little Bob, I mean—why do you grind your grain by hand?"

The driver shrugged. "Have's to make flour, a hey. Bread."

Obviously, none of the machinery was in running order. It was soon obvious that no living Blakeney knew how to mend this, although (said Young Little Bob) there were those who could remember when things were

otherwise: Old Big Mary, Old Little Mary, Old Whitey
Bill—

Hayakawa, with a polite gesture, turned away from
the recitation. "Ezra . . . I think we might be able to fix
all this. Get it in running order. *That* would be something to do, wouldn't it? Something well worth doing.
It would make a big difference."

Ezra said that it would make all the difference.

Shulamith's child, a girl, was born on the edge of a
summer evening when the sun streaked the sky with
rose, crimson, magenta, lime, and purple. "We'll name her
Hope," she said.

"Tongs to make tongs," Mikicho called the work of
repair. She saw the restoration of the water-power as
the beginning of a process which must eventually result
in their being spaceborne again. Robert and Ezra did
not encourage her in this. It was a long labor of work.
They pored and sifted through The House from its
crumbling top to its vast, vast colonnaded cellar, finding
much that was of use to them, much which—though of
no use—was interesting and intriguing—and much which
was not only long past use but whose very usage could
now be no more than a matter of conjecture. They
found tools, metal which could be forged into tools, they
found a whole library of books and they found the
Blakeney-made press on which the books had been
printed; the most recent was a treatise on the diseases
of cattle, its date little more than a hundred years earlier.
Decay had come quickly.

None of the Blakeneys were of much use in the matter of repairs. They were willing enough to lift and move
—until the novelty wore off; then they were only in the
way. The nearest to an exception was Big Fat Red Bob,
the blacksmith; and, as his usual work was limited to

sharpening plowshares, even he was not of much use. Robert and Ezra worked from sunrise to late afternoon. They would have worked longer, but as soon as the first chill hit the air, whatever Blakeneys were on hand began to get restless.

"Have's to get back, now, a hey. Have's to start back."

"Why?" Ezra had asked, at first. "There are no harmful animals on Blakeneyworld, are there?"

It was nothing that any of them could put into words, either clearsound or mumbletalk. They had no tradition of things that go bump in the night, but nothing could persuade them to spend a minute of the night outside the thick walls of The House. Robert and Ezra found it easier to yield, return with them. There were so many false starts, the machinery beginning to function and then breaking down, that no celebration took place to mark any particular day as the successful one. The nearest thing to it was the batch of cakes that Old Big Mary baked from the first millground flour.

"Like longlong times," she said, contentedly, licking crumbs from her toothless chops. She looked at the newcomers, made a face for their baby. A thought occurred to her, and, after a moment or two, she expressed it. "Not ours," she said. "Not ours, you. Elses. But I rather have's you here than that Runaway Little Bob back, or that Thin Jinnie . . . Yes, I rathers."

There was only one serviceable axe, so no timber was cut. But Ezra found a cove where driftwood limbs and entire trees, was continually piling up; and the sawmill didn't lack for wood to feed it. "Makes a lot of boards, a hey," Young Little Bob said one day.

"We're building a house," Robert explained.

The wagoner looked across the bay at the mighty towers and turrets, the great gables and long walls. From the dis-

tance no breach was noticeable, although two of the
chimneys could be seen to slant slightly. "Lots to build,"
he said. "A hey, whole roof on north end wing, mum
mum, bad, it's bad, hey."

"No, we're building our own house."

He looked at them, surprised. "Wants to build another room? Easier, I say, me, clean up a no-one's room.
Oh, a hey, lots of them!"

Robert let the matter drop, then, but it could not be
dropped forever, so one night after eats he began to explain. "We are very grateful for your help to us," he
said, "strangers as we are to you and to your ways.
Perhaps it is because we *are* strange that we feel we want
to have our own house to live in."

The Blakeneys were, for Blakeneys, quiet. They were
also uncomprehending.

"It's the way we've been used to living. On many of
the other worlds people do live, many families—and the
families are all smaller than this, than yours, than the
Blakeneys, I mean—many in one big house. But not on
the world we lived in. There, every family has its own
house, you see. We've been used to that. Now, at first,
all five of us will live in the new house we're going to
build near the mill. But as soon as we can we'll build a
second new one. Then each family will have its own . . ."

He stopped, looked helplessly at his wife and friends.
He began again, in the face of blank nonunderstanding,
"We hope you'll help us. We'll trade our services for
your supplies. You give us food and cloth, we'll grind
your flour and saw your wood. We can help you fix your
furniture, your looms, your broken floors and walls and
roofs. And eventually—"

But he never got to explain about eventually. It was
more than he could do to explain about the new house.

No Blakeneys came to the house-raising. Robert and Ezra fixed up a capstan and hoist, block-and-tackle, managed—with the help of the two women—to get their small house built. But nobody of the Blakeneys ever came any more with grain to be ground, and when Robert and Ezra went to see them they saw that the newly-sawn planks and the lathe-turned wood still lay where it had been left.

"The food we took with us is gone," Robert said. "We have to have more. I'm sorry you feel this way. Please understand, it is not that we don't like you. It's just that we have to live our own way. In our own houses."

The silence was broken by a baby Blakeney. "What's 'houses'?," he asked.

He was shushed. "No such word, hey," he was told, too.

Robert went on, "We're going to ask you to lend us things. We want enough grain and tatoplants and such to last till we can get our own crops in, and enough milk-cattle and draft-animals until we can breed some of our own. Will you do that for us?"

Except for Young Whitey Bill, crouched by the burning, who mumbletalked with "Rower, rower, rower," they still kept silence. Popping blue eyes stared, faces were perhaps more florid than usual, large, slack mouths trembled beneath long hook-noses.

"We're wasting time," Ezra said.

Robert sighed. "Well, we have no other choice, friends . . . Blakeneys . . . We're going to have to take what we need, then. But we'll pay you back, as soon as we can, two for one. And anytime you want our help or service, you can have it. We'll be friends again. We *must* be friends. There are so many, many ways we can help one another to live better—and we are all there are, really, of humanity, on all this planet. We—"

Ezra nudged him, half-pulled him away. They took a wagon and a team of horses, a dray and a yoke of freemartins, loaded up with food. They took cows and ewes, a yearling bull and a shearling ram, a few bolts of cloth, and seed. No one prevented them, or tried to interfere, as they drove away. Robert turned and looked behind at the silent people. But then, head sunk, he watched only the bay road ahead of him, looking aside neither to the water or the woods.

"It's good that they can see us here," he said, later on that day. "It's bound to make them think, and, sooner or later, they'll come around."

They came sooner than he thought.

"I'm so glad to see you, friends!" Robert came running out to greet them. They seized and bound him with unaccustomed hands. Then, paying no attention to his anguished cries of "Why? Why?" they rushed into the new house and dragged out Shulamith and Mikicho and the baby. They drove the animals from their stalls, but took nothing else. The stove was now the major object of interest. First they knocked it over, then they scattered the burning coals all about, then they lit brands of burnwood and scrambled around with them. In a short while the building was all afire.

The Blakeneys seemed possessed. Faces red, eyes almost popping from their heads, they mumble-shouted and raved. When Ezra, who had been working in the shed came running, fighting, they bore him to the ground and beat him with pieces of wood. He did not get up when they were through; it seemed apparent that he never would. Mikicho began a long and endless scream.

Robert stopped struggling for a moment. Caught off-guard, his captors loosened their hold—he broke away from their hands and his bonds, and, crying, "The tools! The tools!", dashed into the burning fire. The blazing roof fell in upon him with a great crash. No sound came from him, nor from Shulamith, who fainted. The baby began a thin, reedy wail.

Working as quickly as they could, in their frenzy, the Blakeneys added to the lumber and waste and scraps around the machinery in the shed, soon had it all ablaze.

The fire could be seen all the way back.

"Wasn't right, wasn't right," Young Red Bob said, over and over again.

"A bad thing," Old Little Mary agreed.

Young Big Mary carried the baby. Shulamith and Mikicho were led, dragging, along. "Little baby, a hey, a hey," she crooned.

Old Whitey Bill was dubious. "Be bad blood," he said. "The elses women grow more babies. A mum mum," he mused. "Teach them better. Not to funnywalk, such." He nodded and mumbled, peered out of the window-look, his loose mouth widening with satisfaction. "Wasn't right," he said. "Wasn't *right*. Another house. Can't be another *house*, a second, a third. Hey, a hey! Never was elses but The House. Never be again. No."

He looked around, his gaze encompassing the cracked walls, sinking floors, sagging roof. A faint smell of smoke was in the air. "The House," he said, contentedly. "The House."

The Power of Every Root

Carlos Rodriguez Nuñez, a police officer of the municipality of Santo Tomas, sat in the private waiting room
of Dr. Olivera considering his situation. Perhaps he ought
not to be there at all.

Not the private waiting room in particular: it was
usually empty except during the week following major
fiestas, when it was likely to be much occupied by the
younger sons of prosperous families who had (the
younger sons) visited the Federal Capital, touring the libraries and theaters and museums and other buildings
of the national patrimony . . . but never, never *las
casitas.* The reason, therefore, why they were here?

"A strain, Sir Doctor. Without doubt, nothing more
than a strain . . . ! Woe of me, Sir Doctor! What an
enormous needle! Surely—just for a tiny, little strain?"

The physician would smile benignly, speak soothingly,
continue charging his syringe with penicillin.

None of this was applicable to the police officer Carlos. In fact, it was not applicable to the younger sons of
the *non*-prosperous families, who—for one thing—could
only afford to visit the District Capital (or, at most, the

State one) on fiestas; and—for another—did not take their
subsequent difficulties to a physician: they took them to
the *curandero*. Carlos now wondered if he should not
do the same. No . . . No . . . The social status of a
government employee, a civil servant, might be imperiled by visiting a native herbalist and wizard. Besides, the physician's public waiting room was just that:
public. Let him be seen there, word would get around,
Don Juan Antonio would ask questions. Don Juan Antonio
was *jefe de policia*, and it seemed to Carlos that his
superior's manner to him of late had lacked cordiality.
But, then, it seemed to Carlos that everybody's attitude
toward him of late lacked cordiality. He could not understand why this should be. He was a very gentle policeman; he took only the customary little bites of graft;
he did not hit drunks hard; he gave cigarettes to prison-
ers. Often.

Why, therefore, people should—suddenly, sometimes
only for matters of a few seconds—change, become hideous, diabolical, when they looked at him, he could not
know. Their faces would swell, become even more horrible than those of the masked *moros* or the judases in the
fiesta parades had seemed to him as a child. The air
would become hot; voices would croak and mutter ugly
things; he had difficulty breathing, sometimes. And his
head—

A large, tinted oval photograph of old Doña Caridad,
Dr. Olivera's mother, glared at him from the wall. Her
lips writhed. She scowled. Carlos got up hastily. Doña
Caridad's unexpected and totally unprovoked hostility
was more than he could stand. He had his hand out to
open the outer door when the inner door opened and
the physician himself stood there—momentarily surprised,
immediately afterwards urbane as always. Bowing him

in. Doña Caridad was as immovable and expressionless as before.

There was a formal exchange of courtesies. Then silence. Dr. Olivera gestured toward a publication on his desk. "I have just been reading," he said, "in the medical journal. About eggs. Modern science has discovered so much about eggs." Carlos nodded. Dr. Olivera placed his fingertips together. He sighed. Then he got up and, with a sympathetic expression, gestured for Carlos to drop his trousers.

"Ah, no, Sir Medico," the officer said hastily. "No, no, it isn't anything like that." Dr. Olivera's mouth sagged. He seemed to hesitate between annoyance and confusion. Carlos breathed in, noisily, then said, all in a rush, "My head is bursting, I have dizziness and pains, my eyes swell, my chest burns, my heart also, and—and—" He paused. He couldn't tell about the way people's faces changed. Or about, just now, for example, Doña Caridad. Dr. Olivera might not be trusted to keep confidence. Carlos choked and tried to swallow.

The physician's expression had grown increasingly reassured and confident. He pursed his lips and nodded. "Does the stomach work?" he inquired. "Frequently? Sufficiently frequently?"

Carlos wanted to tell him that it did, but his throat still was not in order, and all that came out was an uncertain croak. By the time he succeeded in swallowing, the *señor medico* was speaking again.

"Ninety percent of the infirmities of the corpus," he said, making serious, impressive sounds with his nose, "are due to the stomach's functioning with insufficient frequency. Thus the corpus and its system become poisoned. Sir Police Officer—poisoned! We inquire as to the results—We find—" he shook his head rapidly from

side to side and he threw up his hands "—that pains
are encountered. They are encountered not only in the
stomach, but in," he enumerated on his fingers, "the head.
The chest. The eyes. The liver and kidneys. The urological
system. The upper back. The lower back. The legs.
The entire corpus, sir, becomes debilitated." He lowered
his voice, leaned forward, half-whispered, half-hissed,
"One lacks capacity . . ." He closed his eyes, compressed
his lips, and leaned back, fluttering his nostrils and giving short little up-and-down nods of his head. His eyes
flew open, and he raised his brows. *"Eh?"*

Carlos said, "Doctor, I am thirty years old, I have
always until now been in perfect health, able, for example, to lift a railroad tie. My wife is very content.
Whenever I ask her, she says, *¿ Como no?* And afterwards
she says, *Ay, bueno! I* do *not* lack—" A baby cried in
the public waiting room. Dr. Olivera got up and took
out his pen.

"I will give you a prescription for an excellent medication," he said, making a fine flourish and heading the
paper with a large, ornate, *Sr. C. Rodriguez N.* He
wrote several lines, signed it, blotted it, handed it over.
"One before each alimentation for four days, or until
the stomach begins to function frequently . . . Do you
wish the medicine from me, or from the *farmacia?*"

Discouraged, but still polite, Carlos said, "From you,
Doctor. And . . . Your honorarium?"

Dr. Olivera said, deprecatingly, "With the medication
. . . ten pesos. For you, as a civil servant. Thank you
. . . ah! And also: avoid eggs. Eggs are difficult to digest
—they have very, very large molecules."

Carlos left via the private waiting room. Doña Caridad
looked away, contemptuously. Outside, those coarse fel-

lows, woodcutters, the cousins Eugenio and Onofrio
Cruz, nudged one another, sneered. Carlos looked away.

He crossed the plaza, vaguely aware of its smells of
grilling, crisp pork *carnitas,* ripe fruit, wood smoke. His
head and eyes and throat were misbehaving again. He
remembered that the *Forestal* authorities had forbidden
woodcutting for a month as a conservation measure and
that he had meant to look out for possible violations.
A toothless old Indian woman with bare, gray feet, padded
by, mumbling a piece of fried fish. Her face twisted,
became huge, hideous. He shut his eyes, stumbled. After
a moment he felt better and went on up the steps of
the covered market and into the *excusado.* As always
he received mild pleasure from not having to pay the
twenty centavos charge. He closed the door of the booth,
dropped the pills in the bowl, flushed it. So. Saved twenty
centavos, spent—wasted—ten pesos. On the wall was a
new crop of graffiti. *A harlot is the mother of Carlos
Rodriguez N.* read one. Ordinarily he would have read
it without malice, even admiring the neat moderation of
the insult—by crediting him with two family names,
albeit reducing one to the formal initial, the writer had
avoided accusing him of illegitimacy. Or he might have
remarked to himself the effects of enforcing the lowered
compulsory school entrance age: the obscenities were increasingly being written lower and lower on the walls.

But now—now—

Incoherent with rage, he rushed, shouting, outside.
And almost ran into his superior, Don Juan Antonio, the
chief of police. Who looked at him with the peculiar
look so familiar nowadays, asked, "Why are you shouting?" And sniffed his breath.

Accepting this additional insult, Carlos muttered something about boys begging in the market. Don Juan An-

tonio brushed this aside, gestured toward the other end of the plaza. "Twenty auto-buses of students from the high schools and colleges of the State Capital are stopping over here before they continue on to the National Youth Convention. Must I direct traffic myself while you are chasing beggar boys?"

"Ah, no, *señor jefe!*" Carlos walked hastily to where the yellow buses were slowly filing into the plaza and began directing them to the somewhat restricted place available for parking—the rest of the space being already occupied by vendors of black pottery marked with crude fish, brown pottery painted with the most popular women's names, parrot chicks, Tabasco bananas, brightly colored cane-bottom chairs, pineapples sliced open to reveal the sweet contents, shoes, rubber-tire-soled sandals, holy pictures and candles, *rebozos, mantillas,* pear-shaped lumps of farm butter, grilled strips of beef, a hundred varieties of beans, a thousand varieties of chili peppers, work shirts, bright skirts, plastic tablecloths, patriotic pictures, knitted caps, sombreros: the infinite variety of the Latin American marketplace—he called out to the bus driver, banging his hand on the bus to indicate that the vehicle should come back a little bit more . . . a little bit more . . . a little bit—

Crash!

He had backed the bus right into the new automobile belonging to Don Pacifico, the *presidente municipal!* The driver jumped out and cursed; the mayor jumped out and shouted; the students descended; the population assembled; the police chief came running and bellowing; Señorita Filomena—the mayor's aged and virginal aunt —screamed and pressed her withered hands to her withered chest; her numerous great-nephews and great-nieces began to cry—Carlos mumbled, made awkward gestures, and that ox, the stationmaster, a man who notoriously lacked education, and was given to loud public criticism of the police: he laughed.

The crowd became a mob, a hostile mob, the people of which continuously split in two in order to frighten and confuse the miserable police officer with their double shapes and now dreadful faces. It was horrible.

Lupe's body, one was always aware, was altogether independent of Lupe's dress. It did not depend upon it for support, nor did it quarrel or struggle to escape from it, but, firm and smooth and pleasant, it announced both its presence and its autonomy and, like the dress itself, was always bright and clean and sweet. Others might doubt the fidelity of a comely wife, but not Carlos.

Lupe was the best thing about the *ranchito* Rodriguez, but there were other good things about it—everything, in fact, about it was good. The large brown adobe bricks of the walls were well-made, well-cured, well-set in their places; the tiles of the roof neither cracked nor leaked nor slipped. *Pajaritos* hopped about from perch to perch in their wooden cages, chirping and singing, outdone in their bright colors only by the dozens of flowering plants set in little pots or cans. Carlos and Lupe never had to buy corn to make *nixtamal*, the dough for tortillas or tamales; they grew their own, and this supplied them as well with husks to wrap and boil the tamales in, and when the cobs had dried they made good fuel. There was an apple tree and a great tall old piñole which supplied them with blue-gray nuts whose kernels were as sweet as the apples. The goat had always fodder enough, the pig was fine and fat, and half a dozen hens relieved them of any need to depend upon the chancy eggs of the market women. Not the least of the *ranchito's* many amenities was its stand of fleshy maguey cactus whose nectar gave an *aguamiel* from which, mixed with the older and stronger *madre de pulque*, came the delicious and finished milk-colored drink which made it unnecessary for either Carlos or Lupe to patronize the bare and shabby, sour-smelling, fly-ridden *pulquerias*.

True, there were no children, but they had only been married two years. It was Carlos's experienced observation that it sometimes took longer than that before children started arriving, and that once they did start, they generally continued in sufficient quantity.

The *ranchito* was good; it was very, very good—but there was all the difference in the world between being a civil servant with a country place and being a peasant. Lupe's figure, with its small but lovely curves, would become stooped and stringy and prematurely old. Carlos would wear the patched, baggy cottons of the *campesino* instead of his neat gabardines. That is, if he merely lost his job. What costume they wore, those unfortunates in the Misericordia, the great walled hospital for the mentally infirm, he did not know.

This institution, long since secularized, had been originally of religious foundation, and Carlos, remembering that, considered the possibility of discussing his problem with the local priest. He did not consider it long. True, Carlos was a believer, and wore no less than two medals on a golden chain against his strong chest. He never went to church: also true. For one thing, it was not very male to go to church. That was for women. And old men. For another, it was regarded that servants of the secular state should neither persecute nor patronize religious functions. Also, the priest, that amiable and gregarious man, might accidently let slip a wrong word in a wrong ear. Of course it was not to be thought for a moment that he would betray the seal of the confessional. But this—this horror of Carlos's days of late—this was no matter to confess. It was not a sin, it was a misfortune. He could seek the *cura's* friendly counsel no more. That worthy man mingled much with the *caciques*, those of political importance. A single sympathetic reference to "poor Carlos," and "poor Carlos" might find himself displaced in office by a *cacique's* nephew, cousin, brother-in-law—the precise degree of relationship hardly mattered.

Not with Don Juan Antonio's warning words still in his ears.

"One more mistake, young one! Just one more—!"

Carlos blinked. He hadn't realized he'd come so far from town. Behind and to his left was the Holy Mountain, the high hill on which had stood the pyramid in pagan times, from which now sounded the discordant bells of the little church. Behind and to his right was the concrete circle of the bullring. Ahead, the footpath he had for some reason been following broke into a fork. The one to the right led to the little house of his maternal aunt Maria Pilar, a woman of strong personality, who inclined to take advantage of his infrequent visits by asking him to mend her roof or say the rosary or perhaps both. He did not desire to see *Tia* Maria Pilar. Certainly not now. Why, then, was he here?

The path to the left, where did it lead? Eventually to the tiny hamlet of San Juan Bautista. Before that? It paralleled the railroad tracks a long while. It provided access to a well. A small river frequented by washerwomen and occasional gringo artists. Various tracts of woodland. Cornfields. And the isolated house of Ysidro Chache, the *curandero*.

Carlos took off his cap and wiped his forehead. Cautiously, he looked from side to side. Casually, very casually. Far, far off, a tiny figure toiled across the fields leading a laden burro. It was entirely possible that the burro carried a combustible—charcoal, made from illegally cut wood. Or, more simply, the wood itself. Those fellows were so bold! But it was too far away, and besides, that whole matter would wait for another time. What was immediately of concern was that no one, apparently, was observing him, Carlos.

He replaced his cap. Then, still casual—bold, in fact—he turned and took the path to the left.

Ysidro Chache was a wiry, ugly little man with one bad eye, the subject of occasional and uneasy low-toned talk. Could he see out of it, or not? Some held that he could, that, indeed, he could turn his eyes in different directions at once, like a mule. It was also remarked how popular, despite his ugliness, Ysidro Chache was among women. Not ugly ones alone, either. True, he was male. He was very male. In fact, a certain Mama Rosa, shameless, had been heard to say, "Don Ysidro is a bull, and the other men are merely oxen! And he is generous, too . . ."

But the other men had a different explanation. "It is his charms, his love-potions," was the whispered consensus. Often, after such a conversation, more than one man, himself loudly and boastfully male in his *cantina* conversation, would sneak off to the lone small house in the countryside where the healer lived by himself with no steady company except a parrot reputed to be older than the Conquest and to speak all languages; as well as an odd-looking dog which could speak none. Someone, once, had been absurd enough to maintain that this dog came from a breed of barkless ones—but it was known that the man's father had been a foreigner (a Turk, or a Lutheran, or a gringo, or a Jew), and this had added to the absurdity of his contention.

It stood to obvious reason that Ysidro Chache's magic had deprived the dog of his bark in order to demonstrate how clearly he had no need of it to warn him. It was not even fierce! What ordinary person in the world would keep a dog for any other purposes? It was enough to make one shiver!

The path cut into the shoulder of a sloping hill and passed, slowly, by still sturdy though much overgrown stone walls, from the sunlight into the shadow. It was cool in the woods. Perhaps it was no more silent here, perhaps only suddenly it seemed so. Almost, he could wish for the thudding sound of an illicit axe and its flat echo. But he heard none. Only the stealthy movement of something in the underbrush. Then, suddenly, he was at the house. The ancient parrot muttered something, the dog looked up, then down, indifferently. The police officer approached, slowly, announced himself without confidence. No one answered. From somewhere came the sound of a high, weak voice chanting or crooning. The parrot scowled, suddenly became two scowling parrots, but this lasted for only an eye-blink. Carlos was encouraged rather than otherwise . . . it did seem as though the potent influence of the *curandero* and his house was itself sufficient to diminish whatever was wrong with him. He announced himself again and pushed open the door.

The house was dim (naturally, properly) and smelled (not at all dimly) of wood smoke, herbs, rum, and a number of other things, including—recognized at once although for the first time—Ysidro Chache himself.

Who was squatting on the floor, singing his strange song, scattering his colored seeds from a painted gourd onto the floor and examining the pattern in the single thin shaft of sunlight, then scooping up the seeds to cast them down again. Abruptly his song ceased. *"Abuelita*

Ana must die," he said, matter-of-factly. His voice no longer high and weak, but deep and strong.

Carlos tensed. Was the *curandero* intending—Then he remembered who *Abuelita* Ana was, and relaxed. "She has been dying for as long as I can remember her," he said. Grandma Ana, with her twenty layers of garments, her tray of pills and salves and lotions and elixirs, palms and beads and holy pictures, her good luck charms and her patent medicines with the likenesses and signatures of grave and bearded Spanish doctors . . . and most of all, her long and thick and filthy yellow-gray and black fingernails.

Ysidro Chache nodded. "I have been keeping her alive," he said. "But I can't do it any longer. Perhaps today . . . Perhaps tomorrow . . ." He shrugged. "Who knows?"

"And how are you, Sir Healer?"

"I? I am very well. The Lord and the saints love me." He snickered.

Remembering that he was a policeman and that the good offices of a policeman were not despised, Carlos said, "No one has been bothering you, I hope."

The medicine man opened his good and bad eyes very wide. "Bothering *me?* Who would dare?" he said, "but someone has been bothering *you.*"

Carlos Rodriguez Nuñez stared. He sighed, and his sigh broke into a sob. With his voice not always under control, he told the healer of his troubles . . . the ugly voices heard, the ugly faces seen, the pains of body and head, dizziness, doubling of vision, unfriendliness and enmity of people, and—finally—fear that he might lose his job.

Or worse.

The *curandero's* expression, as he listened and nodded

was not totally dissimilar from that of Doctor Olivera. "*Pues* . . . I don't think we have to deal here with the results of impiety," he said slowly, with a reflective air. "You're not a hunter or a woodcutter; you'd have little occasion to offend the Deer people or the Small People . . . even if you had, this is not the way in which they generally take revenge. I say, *generally*. But—for the moment—this is something we'll leave to one side.

"What then? The Evil Eye? One hears a lot of nonsense about it. As a matter of fact, grown men are very rarely the victims of the Evil Eye: it is the children whom one must look out for . . ."

He discussed various possibilities, including malfunctioning of the stomach, or its functioning with insufficient frequency, a difficulty for which he, Ysidro Chache, had many excellent herbs. "But—" the policeman protested, "it is not that. I assure you."

Chache shrugged. "What do you suspect, yourself, then?"

In a low, low voice, Carlos murmured, "Witchcraft. Or, poison."

Chache nodded, slowly, sadly. "Eighty percent of the infirmities of the corpus," he admitted, "proceed from one or the other of these two causes."

"But who—? But why—?"

"Don't speak like an idiot!" the medicine man snapped. "You are a police officer, you have a hundred thousand enemies, and each one has a hundred thousand reasons. *Why* is a little consequence; as for *who*, while it would be helpful if we knew and could lay a counter-curse, it is not essential. We do *not* know *who*, we only know *you*, and it is with *you* that we must concern ourselves."

Humbly, Carlos muttered, "I know. I know."

He watched while Chache cast the seeds again, made

him a *guardero* out of shells and stones and tufts of
bright red wool, censed him with aromatic gum and
fumed him with choking herbs, and performed the other
rituals of the healer's arts, concluding his instructions
with a warning to be exceedingly careful of what he ate
and drank.

The officer threw up his head and hands in despair. "A
man with a thousand eyes could be taken off guard for
long enough—If I turn my head in the cantina for a second, someone could drop a pinch of something into my
food or drink—"

"Then eat only food of your wife's preparing, and as
for drink, I will give you a little charm which will protect
you for either rum or aguardiente."

Vague about the amount of his *honorario,* Chache
would say only that the cost of the first visit was twenty
pesos, including the two charms. He directed that the
next visit be in three days. Carlos walked away feeling
partly reassured and partly re-afraid. The smell of the
magic infumations was still in his nostrils, but, gradually,
in the vanishing day, it was succeeded by others. A haze
hung over everything. Despite official exhortations in the
name of science and patriotism, the ignorant small farmers, and the people of the Indian *ejidos,* whose lands
ringed around the municipality had begun the annual
practice of burning their fields and thickets to prepare
for the corn crop. It was perhaps not the best season,
this one chosen by the *Forestal,* to have forbidden illicit
wood cutting and burning; it would be difficult to dis-
tinguish one smoke from another at any distance—or, at
night, one fire from another. It was a season when the
land seemed to have reverted, in a way, to pagan times;
there was fire all around, and always fire, and not in-
frequently some confused and terrified animal would find

itself cut off, surrounded, and would burn to death. But these offenses against, say, the Deer People, Carlos left to the offending Indios, and to the *curandero*.

Another and lighter haze hung over the town and its immediate environs. It was present twice daily, at early morning and at dusk: the haze of wood and charcoal fires which bore the faint but distinctive odor of tortillas, reminiscent of their faint but distinctive flavor, toasting on griddles. And the *pat-pat-pat* of the hands of the women making them.

Carlos had come to prefer the darkness. In it he could see no hostile, no distorted faces. Seeing fewer objects, he would be disturbed by fewer objects malevolently doubling themselves. If only at such times his irregular pains and distress would diminish as well . . . They seemed to, a little. But a little was not enough. Perhaps the things the *curandero* Ysidro Chache had done would diminish them much. Hastily, furtively, in the gathering darkness, Carlos fell to his knees and said a short, quick prayer to *La Guadalupana.*

It was in his mind that his wife's full name was, after all, Maria de Guadalupe.

"*Tu cafe,*" she said, pouring it as soon as he entered; hot and strong and sweet. "*¿Tu quieres una torta?*"

He proceeded cautiously with his supper at first. But although his sense of taste was distorted, imparting a faintly odd flavor to the food, it seemed that tonight his throat at least would give him no difficulty. Afterwards, as she finished washing the dishes, he approached and embraced her, one arm around her waist, one hand on her breast, and thoughtfully and gently took her ear between his teeth. She said, "*¿Como no?*" as usual.

But afterward she did not, as usual, say, "*¡Ay, bueno!*" And afterward, also, in the bitterness of failure and the fatigue of despair, turning his thoughts to other things, he had his idea.

Surely, if he were to pull off a great coup—arrest someone besides a troublesome *borracho* for a change, for example—surely this would restore his so-greatly fallen credit with the police department, to wit, Don Juan Antonio. At least so he reasoned. He had the vague notion that the plan was not perfect, that, if he considered it carefully, he might find flaws in it. But he didn't wish to consider it that carefully; the effort was too great; there were too many voices muttering ugly things and distracting and bothering him, and besides, if he were to decide against the plan, he would have no reason for getting up. His pains were worse, and he knew he could not get back to sleep again. Therefore he should get up, and if he got up, there was nothing to do but leave the house.

And therefore he might as well try to carry out his plan.

He rose and dressed, buckled on his gun-belt, reassured himself of his flashlight, and went outside.

Dawn was yet not even a promise on the horizon. The stars were great white blazes in the black sky. He searched for Venus, hugest of all, remembering stories of how important she had been in the old religion, before the Conquest—but either she had not yet risen to be the morning star, or he was looking in the wrong place, or some tree or hill obscured her—

He did not need his flashlight yet, knowing the way hereabouts as well as he did his own house, or his own wife. He knew the very tree stump which, suddenly, unkindly . . . but, somehow, not unexpectedly . . . began to croak, "*Carlo' el loco. Carlo' el loco.* Soon you will be encountered in the Misericordia. *¡Ja ja! ¡Loco Carlo'!*"

The officer drew his gun, then thrust it back. A bullet

was undoubtedly of no use. "Wait," he said. "As soon as it is day and I have finished with my other duty, I will return and cut you up and pour *petroleo* on you and burn you up. Wait."

The tree trunk fell silent at once and tried to hide itself in the blackness. But Carlo knew very well where it was, and passed on, giving many grim nods as he thought of it. He strained his ears but heard nothing of what he hoped he might. Doubtless the malefactors had done their original work kilometers away, back in the wooded slopes of the mountains. Deer poachers worked the same territory, usually in pairs, one to hold the bright light to attract and fascinate the animal, and one to shoot it as it stood exposed. One man could carry half a deer easily enough. Such poachers needed neither roads nor paths either coming or going; it was useless to attempt to catch them.

Not so, however, with the woodcutters, those thieves of natural resources and national patrimony, denuding the forested hills and leaving them a prey to erosion! The more he thought of them, the more he realized the iniquity of their crimes. Moreover, look what great rogues they were even when in town—Consider how those cousins Eugenio and Onofrio Cruz (a choice pair!) had sneered and gibbered at him only the day before, in the plaza. In fact, on reflection, not only yesterday, either. And why? For no reason. So, clearly, Carlos's previous attitude had been wrong. Woodcutters were not mere poor devils toiling hard to earn their bread, and currently forbidden even to toil by *burócratas* intent on their own devious ends; merely to confront the axe-men and issue warnings was not enough. The darkness of the woods became overshot with red, scarlet and crimson.

They needed to be taught one good lesson, once and for all. *Ladrones. Hijos de putas.*

But even two men could not carry on their backs enough wood from forest to town to make it worth the effort. A woodcutter required a horse, or a mule, or, at very least, a burro. Which confined him largely to paved or at any rate beaten thoroughfares. There were at least twenty such on this side of the town, but the nearer they approached to town the more they combined, so that, for the practical purposes of the moment, there were only five to be considered. The San Benito road led into the main highway too far south; daylight would find them in the open. The road of the old convent led past a checkpoint. A third was too long and winding; a fourth had in recent months become identical with one of the local creeks. Carlos was not very strong on arithmetic, but he felt fairly certain that this left but one road. To his surprise, he realized that he had, presumably while calculating, reached just that one. It now remained to consider exactly, or even approximately, where on that road might be the best place for his *emboscada.* Too close to the woods, the criminals might escape back into them. Too near the town, they might find refuge in house or patio. An ideal situation would be a place where the road was not only sunken but surrounded by walls on either side, not too near and not too far. Such a situation was not only ideal, it was actual, and it contained, moreover, a niche in which had once reposed an image of La Guadalupana before the Republic was secularized. Carlos snickered, thinking of the astonishment of the rogues as he sprang out upon them from that niche, pistol in hand!

He was still snickering when something seized hold of his foot and sent him sprawling.

The fall jarred his back and all his other bones. It

sickened him, and all his quiescent pains flared up. Voices hooted and gibbered and mocked; faces made horns and spat at him. He lay there in the road, fighting for breath and for reason, sobbing. By and by he was able to breathe. The darkness was only darkness once again. He groped about, his fingers recoiled from what they found, then groped again and found the flashlight. He gave a long, high cry of anguish and of terror at what the yellow beam disclosed lying there in the road: the body of a man lying on its back in a pool of blood. It had shirt and pants and hands and feet, all as a man should.

But where a man's head should be, it had no head.

Slowly, slowly, the sky lightened. Mist mingled with the smoke and obscured the sun. Carlos Rodriguez N., with burning and smarting eyes, paced back and forth in the road. He had been doing so for an hour, two hours, three—who knows how long? He dared not sleep. Suppose someone were to steal the body? He had not dared return to town and report the killing, for the same reason. He had been sustained in his vigil by the certain knowledge that daylight would bring people out on the road, and that he could send one of them into town with his message—preferably one of a group of mature and respectable *ciudadanos* whose testimony about the body would be incontrovertible. But as it happened, the first ones along the road were a pair of boys taking four cows out to pasture.

Or one boy taking two cows. It was no longer possible for Carlos to be sure if he were seeing single or double. One boy and two cows. Two boys and four cows. One body with no head. Two bodies with no heads. The sky was gray and cold and the treacherous sun feared to show itself. Eventually he was satisfied there were two boys, for one of them agreed to run back with the mes-

sage and Carlos could see him running at the same time
he could see the other boy drive the cows off the road so
as to get them past the body. Life or death, the cows must
eat. The boys were out of sight, the cattle, too, and
someone was shouting, still shouting, had been shouting
forever. With a shock, he recognized his own voice, and
fell silent.

Flies began to settle on the blood and on the body.
Very soberly, very tiredly, Carlos observed the corpse.
He did not recognize it. It looked neither familiar nor
strange; it looked merely at rest, with no more problems.
It didn't even seem so odd any more—one had heard
before of murderers removing the heads of their victims
in order to destroy or at least delay identification . . .
Rest. And no problems. How long would it take the boy
to get back to town?—and how long for Don Juan Antonio
to arrive? And then? And what then? Would he commend
Carlos? Curse him? Discharge him? Arrest him? Commit
him?

The man's arms and legs began to tremble. He tried to
repress the tremors, failed, seated himself on a stone,
placed his back against the side of the roadside wall,
placed his revolver in his lap, and without volition or
premonition immediately fell alseep. His head jerked back
and he jumped forward and upward with a cry of alarm,
thrusting his hands forth to catch the revolver. He did
not catch it, neither did he see it fall, neither could he
find it. His shout and motion startled the flies and they
rose from the drying blood with an ugly, thrumming
buzz. Carlos pitched forward onto his hands and knees,
stared stupidly at the dark pool with its blue lights. The
blood was still there.

But the body was gone.

Everything whirled around and around, and Carlos

whirled with it, staggering along the road with arms outstretched to keep from falling. He had slept, he had slept, after the hours of keeping awake to guard the body in the darkness, he had fallen asleep in the earliest daylight! Now he was worse off than ever, for now Don Juan Antonio knew there was a body—and how would Carlos be able to account for its loss? Weeping, sobbing, cursing, stumbling along, he knew that he could account for that no more than for the loss of his revolver. He was certainly doomed.

Unless—Unless—he provided another body, so no one would know the difference.

Below him he saw the railroad tracks. Half-sliding, he descended the slope and ran along the rails. He knew who had, who *must* have done this to him! Who else but the woodcutters, those thieves and sons of harlots? Why else but to take revenge upon him for his intended capture?—and to prevent his ever doing so! But he would show them, now and forever. They had incited the entire *poblacion* against him, but he would show them . . . He came to a switch and just a short distance away was the equipment shed of the maintenance crew, with its weathered inscription: *This Edifice And Its Entire Contents Is The Property Of The Republic.* With his shoulder skewed around he burst it open, seized up the first grass-machete he saw, and rushed out again. He had time? Would he be in time? Would Don Juan Antonio have been awake? Been elsewhere? How soon would he start out? Carlos prayed for time to stand in between Don Juan Antonio and the barbarous plot of the woodcutters.

And luck was with him. The mists parted as he came back over the slope and there down below was a man leading a burro laden with wood. Cautiously and carefully, so shrewdly that he was obliged to smile to himself and to stifle his own laughter, Carlos approached bent over and on crouching knees. The burro approached, the burro passed, Carlos rose to his feet and darted forward on his toes. The machete swung. The body fell, spouting blood. Carlos kicked the fallen head like a football, watched it drop into the underbrush. He threw the body over his shoulder and ran and ran and ran and ran.

"Carlos," said Don Juan Antonio. "Carlos! Do you hear me? Stop that! Stop that and listen to me! Do you hear—"

"No use, *jefe*," said his assistant, Raimundo Cepeda. "It's the shock—the shock. He won't come out of it for a while."

Don Juan Antonio wiped his face with an impeccably ironed and cologne-scented handkerchief. "Not he alone . . . I am also in such a situation. Dreadful. Horrible. People do not realize—"

"Poor young man," sighed the elderly jailor, Uncle Hector, shaking his head. "Only consider—"

Don Juan Antonio nodded vigorously. "By all means let us consider. And let us consider the whole case. Thus I reconstruct it:

"We have the precious pair, the coarsely handsome cousins Eugenio and Onofrio Cruz. Ostensibly and even occasionally woodcutters. On the side—drunkards, when they had the money; thieves . . . and worse . . . when they had the chance. Partners against the rest of the world, fighting often between themselves. Last night they go out to cut wood, illegally. And on the way back a quarrel breaks out. Who knows why? For that matter, perhaps Eugenio merely decided on the spur of the moment to kill Onofrio. At any rate, he *does* kill him, with a blow of his axe. Then, to conceal the identity of the corpus, with the same axe he decapitates it. And returns to his hut, carrying the head. Also, the defunct's wallet.

"Once there, the thought occurs to him that he should not have left the body. With daylight coming, it will soon be found. So he prepares a pile or pyre of wood. With all the burning of fields and thickets, one more smoke will hardly be observed. Should anyone smell anything, they will assume it to be a trapped deer. And he goes back to gain the body. But meanwhile the police have not been idle. Officer Carlos Rodriguez Nuñez is not only up and around, but he has also located the corpus and is guarding it. Eugenio conceals himself. By and by the sun begins to rise, the little brothers Santa Anna approach, and Carlos sends one of them with a message to me. But the child is, after all, only a child; he doesn't go to the right place, wanders around, time is lost. Meanwhile Carlos, content that all will soon be well, sits down and falls asleep. Erroneously," he added, with emphasis, "but—understandably. Understandably.

"Out from his place of concealment creeps the criminal murderer Eugenio Cruz. He steals both Carlos's service revolver *and* the corpus, loads it on the horse which he had brought with him and also concealed at a distance, returns to his hut. There he decides that he has not enough wood to incinerate the victim. So he conceals the corpus inside the hut and goes out for more wood. Meanwhile the unfortunate and valiant Carlos awakens, discovers his loss. By dint of the faculty of raciocination so highly developed in our police, he deduces who the killer must be and where he must have gone. He tracks him down, securing, along the way, a machete. He confronts the arch-criminal. He kills him. Again, I must say: erroneously. And again I must say: understandably. Doubtless the murderer Cruz would have attempted to escape.

"At any rate, this second slaying is witnessed by the

much respected citizen and veteran of the Revolution, Simon-Macabeo Lopez—"

The much respected citizen and veteran of the Revolution, Simon Macabeo Lopez, snapped his sole remaining arm into a salute, and nodded solemnly.

"—who had risen early in order to go and cultivate the piece of land granted him by the grateful Republic. Veteran Lopez immediately and properly proceeds to inform me, arriving at the same time as the little brother Santa Anna. The police at once move to investigate, and we find—that which we found. A body here, a body there, here a head, and there a head, Carlos in a state of incoherent shock. So. Thus my reconstruction. What do you think of it?"

There was a silence. At length the assistant head of the police said, "Masterful. Masterful."

"Thank you."

"It is such a reconstruction, so neat, so lucid, so full of clarity, as is usually to be met with only in the pages of criminal literature. But . . . *señor jefe* . . . it is not the truth. No, I must say, it is not the truth."

Don Juan Antonio snapped, "Why not?"

Cepeda sighed, gestured to the unfortunate Rodriguez. "Because, *señor jefe,* you know and I know and almost everybody in town knows why. That bitch, that strumpet, Lupe de Rodriguez, was cuckolding poor Carlos with the cousins Eugenio and Onofrio Cruz, too. One man was not enough for her. And Carlos was blind to all."

"Truth," said the jailor, sighing.

"Truth," said the veteran, nodding.

"Truth," said the other policemen, shaking their heads, sadly.

Don Juan Antonio glared. Then his expression relaxed, and he lowered his head. "It is the truth," he said, at last. "Ay, Carlos! ¡Woe of me! ¡Hombre! The husband is always the last to learn. For weeks, now, I have scarcely been able to look him in the face. Why, the very honor of the police was imperiled. How the railroad men were laughing at us. Mother!

"So, my poor Carlos—You finally found out, eh? *Nevertheless!*" Don Juan Antonio all but shouted at the others. "It is my reconstruction which must stand, do you agree? Carlos has suffered enough, and moreover, there is the honor of the police."

"Oh, agreed, agreed, *señor jefe*," the other officers exclaimed, hastily and heartily.

"We may depend upon the discretion of the Veteran Lopez, I assume?"

The old man placed his hand over his heart and bowed. "Securely," he said. "What Carlos did may have been, in some sense, technically illegal; I am no scholar, no lawyer. But it was natural. It was male."

"It was male, it was very male," the others all agreed.

Don Juan Antonio bent over, took the weeping Carlos by the shoulder, and tried to reassure him. But Carlos gave no sign of having heard, much less understood. He wept, he babbled, he struck out at things invisible, now and then he gave stifled little cries of alarm and fright and scuttled backwards across the floor. The chief and the others exchanged looks and comments of dismay. "This commences to appear as more than temporary shock," he said. "If he continues like this, he may finally be encountered in the Misericordia, may God forbid. You, Gerardo," he directed the youngest officer, "go and solicit Dr. Olivera to appear as soon as convenient. He understands the techniques of modern science . . . Take no care, Carlos!" he said, encouragingly. "We shall soon have

you perfectly well . . . Now . . . There was something in
my mind . . . Ah, Cepeda."

"Yes, Sir Chief?"

"You said, '. . . with Eugenio and Onofrio Cruz, too.'
Too. Who else? Eh? What other man or men—I insist
that you advise me of their names!"

Rather reluctantly, the assistant said, "Well . . . sir
. . . I know of only one other. Ysidor Chache. The *curandero*."

Astounded, first, then outraged, then determined, Don
Juan Antonio arose to his full height. "The *curandero*,
eh. That mountebank. That whore-monger. That char-
latan." He reached over and took up his cap. "Come. We
will pay a call upon this relic of the past. Let us inform
him that the police have teeth. Eh?"

The jailor, old Hector, shook his head vigorously. The
even older veteran of the Revolution put out his hand.
"No, no, *patron*," he said, imploringly. "Do not go. He
is dangerous. He is very dangerous. He knows all the
spirits and the demons of the woods. He can put a fearful
curse upon you. No, no, no—"

"What!" cried Don Juan Antonio, scornfully. "Do you
think for a moment that I put stock in such superstition?"
He stood brave and erect, not moving from his place.

Old Hector said, "Ah, *patron*. It is not only that. I,
after all, I, too, am a civil servant. I do not—But, sir,
consider. The *curandero* knows the power of every root
and herb and leaf and grass. He is familiar with each
mushroom and toadstool. Consider, consider—a single
pinch in food or drink (and what man has a thousand
eyes?)—Consider the result of such poison! Sterility, im-
potence, abortion, distortion of vision, paralysis of the
throat, imaginary voices, dizziness, pain, swelling of the
eyes, burning of the chest and heart, hallucinations, wast-

ing away, insanity, and who knows what else? No, *patron,* no, no."

"He traffics with the devil," old Lopez muttered, nodding.

"Hm, well," said Don Juan Antonio. "This commences to sound like a matter for the priest, then, would you say?"

"Securely, the priest! If not, indeed, the bishop!"

Instantly the chief of police returned his cap to its place. "Obviously, then, it would be unfitting for a servant of the secular Republic to mix in such a matter. I thank you for calling this to my attention. We shall not dignify the old fraud with our presence."

His eye at that moment was looking out the window. He seemed startled. "Speaking of the—Heh-hem. Did I not mention the good priest? Look." The good priest was indeed at that moment crossing the plaza, his technically illegal cassock covered by an unobjectionable overcoat for most of its length. Preceding him was his sacristan, bearing the small case in which, all knew, were carried the vessels for the administering of last sacrament.

"Hector—do me the favor, go and enquire, who has died?—and then go and see what is keeping the doctor. ¡Ay, Carlos, hombre!"

Hector trotted out. A moment later he returned close enough to call a name before proceeding to the physician's office.

"What did he say?" Don Juan Antonio inquired. "Who?"

"Sir, *Abuelita* Ana. You know, the—"

"What?" Don Juan Antonio was surprised. "*Grandmother* Ana? Who would have expected it? She had been dying as long as I can remember her. Well, well, well . . ." His mouth still astonished, he lifted his right hand and slowly crossed himself.

The Sources of the Nile

It was in the Rutherford office on Lexington that Bob
Rosen met Peter ("Old Pete"—"Sneaky Pete"—"Poor Pete":
take your pick) Martens for the first and almost last
time. One of those tall, cool buildings on Lexington with
the tall, cool office girls it was; and because Bob felt
quite sure he wasn't and damned well never was going
to be tall or cool enough for him to mean anything to
them, he was able to sit back and just enjoy the scenery.
Even the magazines on the table were cool: *Spectator,
Botteghe Oscuro,* and *Journal of the New York State
Geographical Society.* He picked up the last and began
to leaf through "Demographic Study of The Jackson
Whites."

He was trying to make some sense out of a mass of
statistics relating to albinism among that curious tribe
(descended from Tuscorora Indians, Hessian deserters,
London street women, and fugitive slaves), when one of
the girls—delightfully tall, deliciously cool—came to usher
him in to Tressling's office. He lay the magazine face
down on the low table and followed her. The old man
with the portfolio, who was the only other person waiting,

got up just then, and Bob noticed the spot of blood in his eye as he passed by. They were prominent eyes, yellowed, reticulated with tiny red veins, and in the corner of one of them was a bright red blot. For a moment it made Rosen feel uneasy, but he had no time then to think about it.

"Delightful story," said Joe Tressling, referring to the piece which had gotten Rosen the interview, through his agent. The story had won first prize in a contest, and the agent had thought that Tressling . . . if Tressling . . . maybe Tressling . . .

"Of course, we can't touch it because of the theme," said Tressling.

"Why, what's wrong with the Civil War as a theme?" Rosen said.

Tressling smiled. "As far as Aunt Carrie's Country Cheese is concerned," he said, "the South *won* the Civil War. At least, it's not up to Us to tell Them differently. It might annoy Them. The North doesn't *care*. But write another story for us. The Aunt Carrie Hour is always on the lookout for new dramatic material."

"Like for instance?" Bob Rosen asked.

"What the great cheese-eating American public wants is a story of resolved conflict concerning young contemporary American couples earning over ten thousand dollars a year. But nothing sordid, controversial, outré, or passé."

Rosen was pleased to be able to see Joseph Tressling, who was the J. Oscar Rutherford Company's man in charge of scripts for the Aunt Carrie Hour. The *Mené Mené* of the short story was said that year to be on the wall, the magazines were dying like mayflies, and the sensible thing for anyone to do who hoped to make a living writing (he told himself) was to get into television. But he really didn't expect he was going to make the transition, and the realization that he didn't really know any contemporary Americans—young, old, married, single—who were earning over ten thousand dollars a year seemed to prophesy that he was never going to earn it himself.

"And nothing avant-garde," said Tressling.

The young woman returned and smiled a tall, cool smile at them. Tressling got up. So did Bob. "Mr. Martens is still outside," she murmured.

"Oh, I'm afraid I won't be able to see him today," said Joe Tressling. "Mr. Rosen has been so fascinating that the time seems to have run over, and then some. . . . Great old boy," he said, smiling at Bob and shaking his hand. "Really one of the veterans of advertising, you know. Used to write copy for Mrs. Winslow's Soothing Syrup. Tells some fascinating yarns. Too bad I haven't the time to listen. I expect to see you back here soon, Mr. Rosen," he said, still holding Bob's hand as they walked to the door, "with another one of your lovely stories. One that we can feel delighted to buy. No costume dramas, no foreign settings, nothing outré, passé, or avant-garde, and above all—nothing controversial or sordid. You're not going to be one of those *hungry* writers, are you?"

Even before he answered, Rosen observed Tressling's eyes dismiss him; and he resolved to start work immediately on an outré, controversial, sordid costume drama with a foreign setting, etc., if it killed him.

He made the wrong turn for the elevator and on coming back he came face to face with the old man. "'Demography of the Jackson Whites'," the old man said, feigning amazement. "What do you care about those poor suckers for? They don't buy, they don't sell, they don't

start fashion, they don't follow fashion. Just poach, forni-
cate, and produce oh-point-four hydrocephalic albinoes
per hundred. Or something."

The elevator came and they got in together. The old
man stared at him, his yellow-bloody eye like a fertilized
egg. "Not that I blame them," he went on. "If I'd had
any sense I'd've become a Jackson White instead of an
advertising man. The least you can do," he said, without any transition, "is to buy me a drink. Since Truth-
ful Tressling blames it onto you that he can't see me,
the lying bugger. Why, for crying out loud!" he cried.
"What I've got here in this little old portfolio—why,
it's worth more to those men on Madison, Lexington,
Park—if they only—"

"Let me buy you a drink," said Rosen, resignedly. The
streets were hot, and he hoped the bar would be cool.

"A ball of Bushmill," said old Peter Martens.

The bar *was* cool. Bob had stopped listening to his
guest's monologue about what he had in his little old
portfolio (something about spotting fashion trends way
in advance) and had begun talking about his own con-
cerns. By and by the old man, who was experienced
beyond the norm in not being listened to, had begun
to listen to *him*.

"This was when everybody was reading Aku-Aku," Bob
said. "So I thought for sure that mine would go over
good because it was about Rapa Nui—Easter Island—
and Peruvian blackbirders and hints of great legends of
the past and all that."

"And?"

"And it didn't. The publisher, the only one who showed
any interest at all, I mean, *that* publisher, he said *he*
liked the writing but the public wouldn't buy it. He
advised me to study carefully the other paperbacks on

the stands. See what they're like, go thou and do like-
wise. So I did. You know the stuff. On even-numbered
pages the heroine gets her brassiere ripped off while
she cries, 'Yes! Yes! Now! Oh!'"

He was not aware of signalling, but from time to time
a hand appeared and renewed their glasses. Old Martens
asked, "Does she cry 'rapturously'—or 'joyously'?"

"Rapturously *and* joyously. What's the matter, you
think she's frigid?"

Martens perished the thought. At a nearby table a
large blonde said, lugubriously, "You know, Harold, it's
a lucky thing the Good Lord didn't give me any children
or I would of wasted my life on them like I did on my
rotten step-children." Martens asked what happened on
the odd-numbered children.

"I mean, 'pages'," he corrected himself, after a moment.

The right side of Bob Rosen's face was going numb.
The left side started tingling. He interrupted a little
tune he was humming and said, "Oh, the equation is
invariable: On odd-numbered pages the hero either clonks
some bastard bloodily on the noggin with a roscoe, or
kicks him in the collions and *then* clonks him, or else
he's engaged—with his shirt off, you're not allowed to
say what gives with the pants, which are so much more
important: presumably they melt or something—he's engaged, shirtless, in arching his lean and muscular flanks
over some bimbo, *not* the heroine, because these aren't
her pages, some other female in whose pelvis he reads
strange mysteries . . ." He was silent for a moment,
brooding.

"How could it fail, then?" asked the old man, in his
husky voice. "I've seen the public taste change, let me
tell you, my boy, from A Girl of the Limberlost (which
was so pure that nuns could read it) to stuff which

makes stevedores blench: so I am moved to inquire, How could the work you are describing to me fail?"

The young man shrugged. "The nuns were making a come-back. Movies about nuns, books about nuns, nuns on TV, westerns. . . . So the publisher said public taste had changed, and could I maybe do him a life of St. Teresa?"

"Coo."

"So I spent three months doing a life of St. Teresa at a furious pace, and when I finished it turned out I'd done the wrong saint. The simple slob had no idea there was any more than one of the name, and I never thought to ask did he mean the Spanish St. Teresa or the French one? D'Avila or The Little Flower?"

"Saints preserve us. . . . Say, do you know that wonderful old Irish toast? 'Here's to the Council of Trent, that put the fasting on the meat and not on the drink'?"

Bob gestured to the barkeeper. "But I didn't understand why if one St. Teresa could be sold, the other one couldn't. So I tried another publisher, and all *he* said was, public taste had changed, and could I do him anything with a background of juvenile delinquency? After that I took a job for a while selling frozen custard in a penny arcade and all my friends said, BOB! You with *your talent?* How COULD you?"

The large blonde put down a jungle-green drink and looked at her companion. "What you mean, they love me? If they love me why are they going to Connecticut? You don't go to Connecticut if you love a person," she pointed out.

Old Martens cleared his throat. "My suggestion would be that you combine all three of your mysteriously unsalable novels. The hero sails on a Peruvian blackbirder to raid Easter Island, the inhabitants whereof he kicks in the collions, if male, or arches his loins over, if female; until he gets converted by a vision of both St. Teresas who tell him their life stories—as a result of which he takes a job selling frozen custard in a penny arcade in order to help the juvenile delinquents who frequent the place."

Bob grunted. "Depend on it, with my luck I would get it down just in time to see public taste change again. The publishers would want a pocket treasury of the McGuffey Readers, or else the memoirs of Constantine Porphyrogenetus. I could freeze my arse climbing the Himalayas only to descend, manuscript in hand, to find everybody on Publishers' Row vicariously donning goggles and spearing fish on the bottom of the Erythrean Sea. . . . Only thing is, I never was sure to what degree public taste changed by itself or how big a part the publishers play in changing it. . . ."

The air, cool though he knew it was, seemed to shimmer in front of him, and through the shimmer he saw Peter Martens sitting up straight and leaning over at him, his seamed and ancient face suddenly eager and alive. "And would you like to be sure?" old Martens asked. "Would you like to be able to know, really to *know*?"

"What? How?" Bob was startled. The old man's eye looked almost all blood by now.

"Because," Martens said, "*I* can tell you what. *I* can tell you how. Nobody else. Only *me*. And not just about books, about everything. Because—"

There was an odd sort of noise, like the distant sussuration of wind in dry grass, and Rosen looked around and he saw that a man was standing by them and laughing. This man wore a pale brown suit and had a pale brown complexion, he was very tall and very thin and had a very small head and slouched somewhat. He looked like a mantis, and a mustache like an inverted V was cropped out of the broad blue surface of his upper lip.

"Still dreaming your dreams, Martens?" this man asked, still wheezing his dry whispery laugh. "Gates of Horn, or Gates of Ivory?"

"Get the Hell away from me, Shadwell," said Martens.

Shadwell turned his tiny little head to Rosen and grinned. "He been telling you about how he worked on old Mrs. Winslow's Soothing Syrup Account? Too bad the Harrison Narcotics killed that business! He tell you how he worked on the old Sapolio account. The old Stanley Steamer account?" ("Shove off, Shadwell," Martens ordered, planting his elbows in the table and opening his mouth at Bob again.) "Or has he been muttering away like an old Zambezi hand who claims to know the location of the Elephants' Graveyard? Tell me, where is fashion bred?" he intoned. "In the bottle—or in Martens' head?"

Martens' head, thinly covered with yellowish-white hair, jerked in the direction of the new arrival. "This, my boy, is T. Pettys Shadwell, the most despicable of living men. He runs—out of his pocket, because no one will sell him a hat on credit—he runs a so-called market research business. Though who in blazes would hire him since Polly Adler went respectable beats the Hell out of me. I'm warning you, Shadwell," he said, "take off. I've had my fill of you. I'm not giving you any more information." And with a further graphic description of what else he would *not* give T. Pettys Shadwell if the latter was dying of thirst, he folded his arms and fell silent.

The most despicable of living men chuckled, poked a bone-thin hand into a pocket, plucked out a packet of white flaps of cardboard, one of which he tore along a perforated line and handed to Bob. "My card, sir. My operation, true, is not large, but it is Ever Growing. Don't take Mr. Martens too seriously. And don't buy him too many drinks. His health is not as good as it used to be—and then, it never was." And with a final laugh, like the rustling of dried corn-shucks, he angled away.

Martens sighed, lapped the last few dewy drops of Bushmill's off a molten ice-cube. "I live in mortal fear that some day I'll have the money to buy all the booze I want and wake up finding I have spilled the beans to that cockatrice who just walked out. Can you imagine anyone having business cards printed to be torn off of perforated pads? Keeps them from getting loose and wrinkled, is his reason. Such a man has no right, under natural or civil law, to live."

In the buzzing coolness of the barroom Bob Rosen tried to catch hold of a thought which was coyly hiding behind a corner in his mind. His mind otherwise, he felt, was lucid as never before. But somehow he lost the thought, found he was telling himself a funny story in French and—although he had never got more than an 80 in the course, back in high school—marvelled at the purity of his accent and then chuckled at the punchline.

"'Never mind about black neglijays,'" the stout blonde was saying. "'If you want to keep your husband's affections,' I said to her, 'then listen to me—'"

The errant thought came trotting back for reasons of its own, and jumped into Bob's lap. "'Spill the beans'?" he quoted, questioningly. "Spill *what* beans? To Shadwell, I mean."

"Most despicable of living men," said old Martens, mechanically. Then a most curious expression washed over his antique countenance: proud, cunning, fearful . . .

"Would you like to know the sources of the Nile?" he asked. "Would you?"

"'Let him *go* to Maine,' I said. 'Let him paint rocks all day,' I said. 'Only for Heaven's sake, keep him the Hell off of Fire Island,' I said. And was I right, Harold?" demanded the large blonde.

Pete Martens was whispering something, Bob realized. By the look on his face it must have been important, so the young man tried to hear the words over the buzzing, and thought to himself in a fuddled fashion that they ought to be taken down on a steno pad, or something of that sort . . . *want to know, really know, where it begins and how, and how often?* But no; what do I know? For years I've been Clara the rotten stepmother, and now I'm Clara the rotten mother-in-law. *Are there such in every generation? Must be . . . known for years . . . known for years . . . only, Who?—and Where?—searched and sought, like Livingston and all the others searching and seeking, enduring privation, looking for the sources of the Nile . . .*

Someone, it must have been Clara, gave a long, shuddering cry; and then for a while there was nothing but the buzzing, buzzing, buzzing, in Bob Rosen's head; while old Martens lolled back in the chair, regarding him silently and sardonically with his blood-red eye, over which the lid slowly, slowly drooped: but old Martens never said a word more.

It was one genuine horror of a hangover, subsiding slowly under (or perhaps despite) every remedy Bob's aching brain could think of: black coffee, strong tea, chocolate milk, raw-egg-red-pepper-worcestershire sauce. At least, he thought gratefully after a while, he was spared the dry heaves. At least he had all the fixings in his apartment and didn't have to go out. It was a pivotal neighborhood, and he lived right in the pivot, a block where lox and bagels beat a slow retreat before the advance of hog maw and chitterlings on the one hand and *bodegas, comidas criollas,* on the other; swarms of noisy kids running between the trucks and buses, the jackhammers forever wounding the streets.

It took him a moment to realize that the noise he was hearing now was not the muffled echo of the drills, but a tapping on his door. Unsteadily, he tottered over and opened it. He would have been not in the least surprised to find a raven there, but instead it was a tall man, rather stooping, with a tiny head, hands folded mantis-like at his bosom.

After a few dry, futile clickings, Bob's throat essayed the name "Shadburn?"

"Shadwell," he was corrected, softly. "T. Pettys Shadwell . . . I'm afraid you're not well, Mr. Rosen . . ."

Bob clutched the doorpost, moaned softly. Shadwell's hands unfolded, revealed—not a smaller man at whom he'd been nibbling, but a paper bag, soon opened.

". . . so I thought I'd take the liberty of bringing you some hot chicken broth."

It was gratefully warm, had both body and savor. Bob lapped at it, croaked his thanks. "Not at all, not-a-tall," Shadwell waved. "Glad to be of some small help." A silence fell, relieved only by weak, gulping noises. "Too bad about old Martens. Of course, he *was* old. Still, a shocking thing to happen to you. A stroke, I'm told. I, uh, trust the police gave you no trouble?"

A wave of mild strength seemed to flow into Bob from the hot broth. "No, they were very nice," he said. "The sergeant called me, 'Son.' They brought me back here."

"Ah." Shadwell was reflective. "He had no family. I know that for a fact."

"Mmm."

"But—assume he left a few dollars. Unlikely, but— And assume he'd willed the few dollars to someone or some charity, perhaps. Never mind. Doesn't concern us. He wouldn't bother to will his papers . . . scrapbooks of old copy he'd written, so forth. That's of no interest to people in general. Just be thrown out or burned. But it would be of interest to *me*. I mean, I've been in advertising all my life, you know. Oh, yes. Used to distribute handbills when I was a boy. Fact."

Bob tried to visualize T. Pettys Shadwell as a boy, failed, drank soup. "Good soup" he said. "Thanks. Very kind of you."

Shadwell urged him strongly not to mention it. He chuckled. "Old Pete used to lug around some of the darndest stuff in that portfolio of his," he said. "In fact, some of it referred to a scheme we were once trying to work out together. Nothing came of it, however, and the old fellow was inclined to be a bit testy about that, still —I believe you'd find it interesting. May I show you?"

Bob still felt rotten, but the death wish had departed. "Sure," he said. Shadwell looked around the room, then at Bob, expectantly. After a minute he said, "Where is it?" "Where is what?" "The portfolio. Old Martens'."

They stared at each other. The phone rang. With a wince and a groan, Bob answered. It was Noreen, a girl with pretensions to stagecraft and literature, with whom he had been furtively lecherous on an off-and-on basis, the off periods' commencements being signaled by the presence in Noreen's apartment of Noreen's mother, (knitting, middleclass morality and all) when Bob came, intent on venery.

"I've got a terrible hangover," he said, answering her first (guarded and conventional) question; "and the place is a mess."

"See what happens if I turn my back on you for a minute?" Noreen clucked, happily. "Luckily, I have neither work nor social obligations planned for the day, so I'll be right over."

Bob said, "Crazy!", hung up, and turned to face Shadwell, who had been nibbling the tips of his prehensile fingers. "Thanks for the soup," he said, in tones of some finality.

"But the portfolio?" "I haven't got it." "It was leaning against the old man's chair when I saw the two of you in the bar." "Then maybe it's still *in* the bar. Or in the hospital. Or maybe the cops have it. But—" "It isn't. They don't." "But *I* haven't got it. Honest, Mr. Shadwell, I appreciate the soup, but I don't know where the Hell—"

Shadwell rubbed his tiny, sharp mustache, like a Λ-mark pointing to his tiny, sharp nose. He rose. "This is really too bad. Those papers referring to the business old Peter and I had been mutually engaged in—really, I have as much right to them as . . . But look here. Perhaps he may have spoken to you about it. He always did when he'd been drinking and usually did even when he wasn't. What he liked to refer to as, 'The sources of the Nile'? Hmm?" The phrase climbed the belfry and rang bells audible, or at least apparent, to Shadwell. He seemed to leap forward, long fingers resting on Bob's shoulders.

"You do know what I mean. Look. You: Are a writer. The old man's ideas aren't in your line. I: Am an advertising man. They are in my line. For the contents of his portfolio—as I've explained, they are rightfully mine

—I will give: One thousand: Dollars. In fact: For the opportunity of merely *looking* through it: I will give: One *hundred*. Dollars."

As Bob reflected that his last check had been for $17.72 (Monegasque rights to a detective story), and as he heard these vasty sums bandied about, his eyes grew large, and he strove hard to recall what the Hell *had* happened to the portfolio—but in vain.

Shadwell's dry, whispery voice took on a pleading note. "I'm even willing to pay you for the privilege of discussing your conversation with the old f— the old gentleman. Here—" And he reached into his pocket. Bob wavered. Then he recalled that Noreen was even now on her way uptown and crosstown, doubtless bearing with her, as usual, in addition to her own taut charms, various tokens of exotic victualry to which she—turning her back on the veal chops and green peas of childhood and suburbia—was given: such as Shashlik makings, *lokoumi,* wines of the warm south, *baklava, provalone,* and other living witnesses to the glory that was Greece and the grandeur that was Rome.

Various hungers, thus stimulated, began to rise and clamor, and he steeled himself against Shadwell's possibly unethical and certainly inconveniently timed offers.

"Not now," he said. Then, throwing delicacy to the winds, "I'm expecting a girl friend. Beat it. Another time."

Annoyance and chagrin on Shadwell's small face, succeeded by an exceedingly disgusting leer. "Why, of *course,*" he said. "Another time? Certainly. My card—" He hauled out the perforated pack. "I already got one," Bob said. "Goodbye."

He made haste to throw off the noisome clothes in which he had been first hot, then drunk, then comatose; to take a shower, comb his mouse-colored hair, shave the pink bristles whose odious tint alone prevented him from growing a beard, to spray and anoint himself with various nostra which T. Pettys Shadwell's more successful colleagues in advertising had convinced him (by a thousand ways, both blunt and subtle) were essential to his acceptance by good society; then to dress and await with unconcealed anticipation the advent of the unchaste Noreen.

She came, she kissed him, she prepared food for him: ancient duties of women, any neglect of which is a sure and certain sign of cultural decadence and retrogression. Then she read everything he had written since their last juncture, and here she had some fault to find.

"You waste too much time at the beginning, in description," she said, with the certainty possible to those who have never sold a single manuscript. "You've got to make your characters come *alive*—in the very first sentence."

"'Marley was dead, to begin with,'" muttered Bob.

"What?" murmured Noreen, vaguely, feigning not to hear. Her eye, avoiding lover boy, lit on something else. "What's this?" she asked. "You have so much money you just leave it lying around? I thought you said you were broke." And Bob followed her pointing and encarnadined fingertip to where lay two crisp twenty-dollar bills, folded lengthwise, on the table next the door.

"Shadwell!" he said, instantly. And, in response to her arched brows (which would have looked much better unplucked, but who can what will away?), he said, "A real rat of a guy—a louse, a boor—who had some crumby proposal."

"And who also has," said Noreen, going straight to the heart of the matter, "money." Bob resolved never to introduce the two of them, if he could help it. "Anyway," she continued, laying aside Bob's manuscript, "now you can take me out somewhere." Feebly he argued the food then cooking; she turned off the gas and thrust the pots incontinently into the ice-box, rose, and indicated she was now ready to leave. He had other objections to leaving just then, which it would have been impolitic to mention, for in Noreen's scheme of morality each episode of passion was a sealed incident once it was over, and constituted no promise of any other yet to come.

With resignation tempered by the reflection that Shadwell's four sawbucks couldn't last forever, and that there was never so long-drawn-out an evening but would wind up eventually back in his apartment, Bob accompanied her out the door.

And so it was. The next day, following Noreen's departure in mid-morning, found Bob in excellent spirits but flat-broke. He was reviewing the possibilities of getting an advance from his agent, Stuart Emmanuel, a tiny, dapper man whose eyes behind double lenses were like great black shoebuttons, when the phone rang. ESP or no ESP, it was Stuart himself, with an invitation to lunch.

"I'm glad *some* of your clients are making money," said Bob, most ungraciously.

"Oh, it's not my money," said Stuart. "It's J. Oscar Rutherford's. One of his top men—no, it's not Joe Tressling, I know you saw him the day before yesterday, yes, I know nothing came of it, this is a different fellow altogether. Phillips Anhalt. I want you to come."

So Bob left yesterday's half-cooked chow in the icebox and, very little loath, set out to meet Stuart and Phillips Anhalt, of whom he had never heard before. The first rendezvous was for a drink at a bar whose name also meant nothing to him, though as soon as

he walked in he recognized it as the one where he had
been the day before yesterday, and this made him uneasy—doubly so, for he had callously almost forgotten
what had had happened there. The bartender, it was
at once evident, had not. His wary glance at the three
of them must have convinced him that they were reasonably good insurance risks, however, for he made no
comment.

Anhalt was middle-sized man with a rather sweet and
slightly baffled face and iron-gray haircut *en brosse.* "I
enjoyed your story very much," he told Bob—thus breaking in at once upon the shallow slumber of the little
scold who boarded in Bob's Writer's Consciousness. Of
course (it shrilled) I know *exactly* the one you mean,
after all, I've written only *one* story in my entire *life*
so "*your story*" is the only identification it needs. I liked
your *novel*, Mr. Hemingway. I enjoyed your *play*, Mr.
Kaufman.

Stuart Emmanuel, who knew the labyrinthine ways
of writers' mind as he knew the figures in his bank
statement, said smoothly, "I expect Mr. Anhalt refers
to *Unvexed to the Sea.*"

With firm politeness Mr. Anhalt disappointed this
expectation. "I know that's the prize-winner," he said,
"and I mean to read it, but the one I referred to was
The Green Wall." Now, as it happened this very short
little story had been bounced thirteen times before its
purchase for a negligible sum by a low-grade salvage
market of a magazine; but it was one of Bob's favorites.
He smiled at Phillips Anhalt, Anhalt smiled at him,
Stuart beamed and ordered drinks.

The waiter passed a folded slip of paper to Bob Rosen
when he came with the popskull. "The lady left it," he
said. "What lady?" "The blond lady." Agent and ad

man smiled, made appropriate remarks while Bob scanned
the note, recognized it as being in his own handwriting,
failed to make it out, crammed it in his pocket.

"Mr. Anhalt," said Stuart, turning dark, large-pupiled
eyes on his client, is a very important man at Rutherford's:
he has a corner office." A gentle, somewhat tired smile
from Anhalt, who gave the conversation a turn and talked
about his home in Darien, and the work he was doing
on it, by himself. Thus they got through the round of
drinks, then walked a few blocks to the restaurant.

Here Bob was infinitely relieved that Anhalt did not
order poached egg on creamed spinach, corned beef
hash, or something equally simple, wholesome, and disgusting, and tending to inhibit Bob's own wide-ranging
tastes: Anhalt ordered duckling, Stuart had mutton
chops, and Bob chose tripe and onions.

"Joe Tressling tells me that you're going to write something for the cheese show," said Anhalt, as they dis-
arranged the pickle plate. Bob half-lifted his eyebrows,
smiled. Stuart gazed broodingly into the innards of a
sour tomato as if he might be saying to himself, "Ten
percent of $17.72, Monegasque rights to a detective story."

"More cheese is being eaten today in the United States
than twenty-five years ago," Anhalt continued. "Much,
much more. . . . Is it the result of advertising? Such
as the Aunt Carrie Hour? Has that changed public taste?
Or—has public taste changed for, say, other reasons, and
are we just riding the wave?"

"The man who could have answered that question,"
Bob said, "died the day before yesterday."

Anhalt let out his breath. "How do you know he could
have?"

"He said so."

Anhalt, who'd had a half-eaten dilled cucumber in

his hand, carefully laid it in the ash-tray, and leaned forward. "What else did he say? Old Martens, I mean. You *do* mean Old Martens, don't you?"

Bob said that was right, and added, with unintentional untruthfulness, that he'd been offered a thousand dollars for that information, and had turned it down. Before he could correct himself, Anhalt, customary faint pink face gone almost red, and Stuart Emmanuel, eyes glittering hugely, said with one voice, *"Who offered—?"*

"What comes out of a chimney?"

Stuart, recovering first (Anhalt continued to stare, said nothing, while the color receded), said, "Bob, this is not a joke. That is the reason we have this appointment. An awful lot of money is involved—for you, for me, for Phil Anhalt, for, well, for everybody. For just everybody. So—"

It slipped out. "For T. Pettys Shadwell?" Bob asked.

The effect, as they used to say in pre-atomic days, was electrical. Stuart made a noise, between a moan and a hiss, rather like a man who, having trustingly lowered his breeches, sits all unawares upon an icicle. He clutched Bob's hand. "You didn't godforbid *sign* anything?" he wailed. Anhalt, who had gone red before, went white this time around, but still retained diffidence enough to place his hand merely upon Bob's jacket cuff.

"He's a cad!" he said, in trembling tones. "A swine, Mr. Rosen!"

"'The most despicable of living men,'" quoted Mr. Rosen. ("Exactly," said Anhalt.)

"Bob, you didn't *sign* anything, godforbid?"

"No. No. No. But I feel as if I've had all the mystery I intend to have. And unless I get Information, why, gents, I shan't undo one button." The waiter arrived with the food and, according to the rules and customs of the Waiters' Union, gave everybody the wrong orders. When this was straightened out, Stuart said, confidently, "Why, of course, Bob: Information: Why, certainly. There is nothing to conceal. Not from *you*," he said, chuckling. "Go ahead, start eating. I'll eat and talk, you just eat and listen."

And so, as he tucked away the tripe and onions, Bob heard Stuart recount, through a slight barrier of masticated mutton-chop, a most astonishing tale. In every generation (Stuart said) there were leaders of fashion, arbiters of style. At Nero's court, Petronius. In Regency England, Beau Brummel. At present and for some time past, everyone knew about the Paris designers and their influence. And in the literary field ("Ahah!" muttered Bob, staring darkly at his forkful of stewed ox-paunch) —in the literary field, said Stuart, swallowing in haste for greater clarity, they all knew what effect a review by any one of A Certain Few Names, on the front page of the Sunday Times book section, could have upon the work of even an absolute unknown.

"It will sky-rocket it to Fame and Fortune with the speed of light," said Stuart.

"Come to the point." But Stuart, now grinding away on a chunk of grilled sheep, could only gurgle, wave his fork, and raise his eyebrows. Anhalt stopped his moody task of reducing the duckling to a mass of orange-flavored fibres, and turned to take the words, as it were, from Stuart's mutton-filled mouth.

"The point, Mr. Rosen, is that poor old Martens went up and down Madison Avenue for years claiming he had found a way of predicting fashions and styles, and nobody believed him. Frankly, *I* didn't. But I do now. What caused me to change my mind was this: When I heard, day before yesterday, that he had died so suddenly, I had a feeling that I *had* something of his, something that he'd left for me to look at once, something I'd taken just to get rid of him. And, oh, perhaps I was feeling a bit guilty, certainly a bit sorry, so I asked my secretary to get it for me. Well, you know, with the J. Oscar Rutherford people, as with Nature, nothing is ever lost—" Phillips Anhalt smiled his rather shy, rather sweet and slightly baffled smile—"so she got it for me and I took a look at it. . . . I was . . ." he paused, hesitated for *mot juste.*

Stuart, with a masterful swallow, leaped into the breach, claymore in hand. "He was flabbergasted!"

Astounded, amended Anhalt. He was astounded.

There, in an envelope addressed to Peter Martens, and postmarked November 10, 1945, was a color snapshot of a young man wearing a fancy weskit.

"Now, you know, Mr. Rosen, no one in 1945 was wearing fancy weskits. They didn't come in till some years later. How did Martens *know* they were going to come in? And there was another snapshot of a young man in a charcoal suit and a pink shirt. Nobody was wearing that outfit in '45 . . . I checked the records, you see, and the old gentleman had left the things for me in December of that year. I'm ashamed to say that I had the receptionist put him off when he called again . . . But just think of it: fancy weskits, charcoal suits, pink shirts, in 1945." He brooded. Bob asked if there was anything about gray flannel suits in the envelope, and Anhalt smiled a faint and fleeting smile.

"Ah, Bob, now, Bob," Stuart pursed his mouth in mild (and greasy) reproof. "You still don't seem to realize that this is S°E°R°I°O°U°S°."

"Indeed it is," said P. Anhalt. "As soon as I told Mac about it, do you know what he said, Stu? He said,

'Phil, don't spare the horses.'" And they nodded soberly, as those who have received wisdom from on high.

"Who," Bob asked, "is Mac?"

Shocked looks. Mac, he was told, the older men speaking both tandem and *au pair,* was Robert R. Mac Ian, head of the happy J. Oscar Rutherford corporate family.

"Of course, Phil," Stuart observed, picking slyly at his baked potato, "I won't ask why it took you till this morning to get in touch with me. With some other outfit, I might maybe suspect that they were trying to see what they could locate for themselves without having to cut our boy, here, in for a slice of the pie. He being the old man's confidante and moral heir, anyway, so to speak." (Bob stared at this description, said nothing. Let the thing develop as far at it would by itself, he reflected.) "But not the Rutherford outfit. It's too big, too ethical, for things like that." Anhalt didn't answer.

After a second, Stuart went on, "Yes, Bob, this is really something big. If the late old Mr. Martens' ideas can be successfully developed—and I'm sure Phil, here will not expect you to divulge until we are ready to talk Terms—they will be really invaluable to people like manufacturers, fashion editors, designers, merchants, and, last but not least—advertising men. Fortunes can literally be made, and saved. No wonder that a dirty dog like this guy Shadwell is trying to horn in on it. Why, listen— but I'm afraid we'll have to terminate this enchanting conversation. Bob has to go home and get the material in order—" (What material? Bob wondered. Oh, well, so far: $40 from Shadwell and a free lunch from Anhalt.) —"and you and I, Phil, will discuss those horses Mac said not to spare."

Anhalt nodded. It seemed obvious to Rosen that the ad man was unhappy, unhappy about having given Peter Martens the brush-off while he was alive, unhappy about being numbered among the vultures now that he was dead. And, so thinking, Bob realized with more than a touch of shame, that he himself was now numbered among the vultures; and he asked about funeral arrangements. But it seemed that the Masonic order was taking care of that: the late Peter Martens was already on his way back to his native town of Marietta, Ohio, where his lodge brothers would give him a formal farewell: aprons, sprigs of acacia, and all the ritual appurtenances. And Bob thought, why not? And was feeling somehow, very much relieved.

On the uptown bus which he had chosen over the swifter, hotter, dingier subway, he tried to collect his thoughts. What on earth could he ever hope to remember about a drunken conversation, which would make any sense to anybody, let alone be worth money? "The Sources of the Nile," the old man had said, glaring at him with bloody eye. Well, Shadwell knew the phrase, too. Maybe Shadwell knew what it meant, exactly what it meant, because he, Bob Rosen, sure as Hell didn't. But the phrase did catch at the imagination. Martens had spent years—who knew how many?—seeking the sources of his particular Nile, the great river of fashion, as Mungo Park, Livingstone, Speke, and other half-forgotten explorers, had spent years in search of theirs. They had all endured privation, anguish, rebuffs, hostility . . . and in the end, just as the quest had killed Mungo Park, Livingstone, Speke, the other quest had killed old Peter Martens.

But, aside from insisting that there *was* a source or sources, and that he knew *where*, what had Peter said?

Why hadn't Bob stayed sober? Probably that fat blonde at the next table, she of the poisonously green drink and the rotten step-children, probably she retained more of the old man's tale, picked up by intertable osmosis, than did Bob himself.

And with that he heard the voice of the waiter at the bar that noon: *The lady left it . . . What lady? . . . The blond lady . . .* Bob scrabbled in his pocket and came up with the note. On the sweaty, crumpled bit of paper, scrawled in his own writing, or a cruel semblance of it, he read: *Ditx sags su Bimsoh oh—*

"What the *Hell!*" he muttered, and fell to, with furrowed face, to make out what evidently owed more to Bushmill's than to Everhard Faber. At length he decided that the note read, *Peter says, see Bensons on Purchase Place, the Bronx, if I don't believe him. Peter says, write it down.*

"It must mean something," he said, half-aloud, staring absently from Fifth Avenue to Central Park, as the bus roared and rattled between opulence and greenery. "It has to mean something."

"Well, what a shame," said Mr. Benson. "But how nice it was of you to come and tell us." His wavy-gray hair was cut evenly around in soupbowl style, and as there was no white skin at the back of his neck, had evidently been so cut for some time. "Would you like some iced tea?"

"Still, he Went Quickly," said Mrs. Benson, who, at the business of being a woman, was in rather a large way of business. "I don't think there's any iced tea, Daddy. When I have to go, that's the way I want to go. Lemonade, maybe?"

"There isn't any lemonade if what Kitty was drinking was the last of the lemonade. The Masons give you a nice funeral. A real nice funeral. I used to think about joining up, but I never seem to get around to it. I think there's some gin. Isn't there some gin, Mommy? How about a nice cool glass of gin-and-cider, Bob? Kit will make us some, by and by."

Bob said, softly, that that sounded nice. He sat half-sunken in a canvas chair in the large, cool living-room. A quarter of an hour ago, having found out with little difficulty *which* house on Purchase Place was the Bensons', he had approached with something close to fear and trembling. Certainly, he had been sweating in profusion. The not-too-recently painted wooden house was just a blind, he told himself. Inside there would be banks of noiseless machines into which cards were fed and from which tapes rolled in smooth continuity. And a large, broad-shouldered young man whose hair was cut so close to the skull that the scars underneath were plain to see, this young man would bar Bob's way and, with cold, calm, confidence, say, "Yes?"

"Er, um, Mr. Martens told me to see Mr. Benson."

"There is no Mr. Martens connected with our organization and Mr. Benson had gone to Washington. I'm afraid you can't come in: everything here is Classified."

And Bob would slink away, feeling Shoulders' scornful glance in the small of his shrinking, sweaty back.

But it hadn't been like that at all. Not anything like that at all.

Mr. Benson waved an envelope at Bob. "Here's a connivo, if you like," he said. "Fooled I don't know how many honest collectors, and dealers, too: Prince Abu-Somebody flies over here from Pseudo-Arabia without an expense account. Gets in with some crooked dealers, *I* could name them, but I won't, prints off this *en–tire* issue of airmails, precancelled. Made a mint. Flies back to Pseudo-Arabia, *whomp!* they cut off his head!" And he chuckled richly at the thought of this prompt and summary vengeance. Plainly, in Mr. Benson's eyes, it had been done in the name of philatelic ethics; no considerations of dynastic intrigues among the petrol pashas entered his mind.

"Kitty, are you going to make us some cold drinks?" Mrs. B. inquired. "Poor old Pete, he used to be here for Sunday dinner on and off, oh, for just years. Is that Bentley coming?"

Bob just sat and sucked in the coolness and the calm and stared at Kitty. Kitty had a tiny stencil cut in the design of a star and she was carefully lacquering her toenails with it. He could hardly believe she was for real. "Ethereal" was the work for her beauty, and "ethereal" was the only word for it. Long, long hair of an indescribable gold fell over her heart-shaped face as she bent forward towards each perfectly formed toe. And she was wearing a dress like that of a child in a Kate Greenaway book.

"Oh, Bentley," said B., Senior. "What do you think has happened? Uncle Peter Martens passed away, all of a sudden, day before yesterday, and this gentleman is a friend of his and came to tell us about it; isn't that thoughtful?"

Bentley said, "*Ahhh.*" Bentley was a mid-teener who wore jeans cut off at the knees and sneakers with the toes, insteps, and heels removed. He was naked to the waist and across his suntanned and hairless chest, in a neat curve commencing just over his left nipple and terminating just under his right nipple, was the word *VI-PERS* stenciled in red paint.

"*Ahhh,*" said Bentley Benson. "Any pepsies?"

"Well, I'd asked you to bring some," his mother said, mildly. "Make a nice, big pitcher of gin-and-cider, Bentley, please, but only a *little* gin for yourself, in a separate glass, remember, now." Bentley said, "*Ahhh*," and departed, scratching on his chest right over the bright, red *S*.

Bob's relaxed gaze took in, one by one, the pictures in the mantelpiece. He sat up a bit, pointed. "Who is that?" he asked. The young man looked something like Bentley and something like Bentley's father.

"That's my oldest boy, Barton, Junior," said Mother B. "You see that nice vest he's wearing? Well, right after the War, Bart, he was in the Navy then, picked up a piece of lovely brocade over in Japan, and he sent it back home. I thought of making a nice bed-jacket out of it, but there wasn't enough material. So I made it into a nice vest, instead. Poor old Uncle Peter, he liked that vest, took a picture of Bart in it. Well, what do you know, a few years later fancy vests became quite popular, and, of course, by that time Bart was tired of his ("Of course," Bob murmured), so he sold it to a college boy who had a summer job at Little and Harpey's. Got $25 for it, and we all went out to dinner down town that night."

Kitty delicately stenciled another star on her toenails.

"I see," Bob said. After a moment, "Little and Harpey's?" he repeated

Yes, that same. The publishers. Bart, and his younger brother Alton, were publishers' readers. Alt had been with Little and Harpey but was now with Scribbley's Sons; Bart had worked for Scribbley's at one time, too. "They've been with *all* the biggest publishing houses," their mother said, proudly. "Oh, *they* aren't any of your stick-in-the-muds, no sirree." Her hands had been fiddling with a piece of bright cloth, and then, suddenly, cloth and hands went up to her head, her fingers flashed, and—

complete, perfect—she was wearing an intricately folded turban.

Bentley came in carrying a pitcher of drink in one hand and five glasses—one to each finger—in the other. "I told you to mix yours separately, I think," his mother said. Taking no notice of her youngest's *Ahhh*, she turned to Bob. "I have a whole basket of these pieces of madras," she said, "some silk, some cotton . . . and it's been on my mind all day. Now, if I just remember the way those old women from the West Indies used to tie them on their heads when I was girl . . . and now, sure enough, it just came back to me! How does it look?" she asked.

"Looks very nice, Mommy," said Bart, Sr. And added, "I bet it would cover up the curlers better than those babushkas the women wear, you know?"

Bob Rosen bet it would, too.

So here it was and this was it. The sources of the Nile. How old Peter Martens had discovered it, Bob did not know. By and by, he supposed, he would find out. How did they *do* it, was it that they had a *panache*—? or was it a "wild talent," like telepathy, second sight, and calling dice or balls? He did not know.

"Bart said he was reading a real nice manuscript that came in just the other day," observed Mrs. Benson, dreamily, over her glass. "About South America. He says he thinks that South America has been neglected, and that there is going to be a revival of interest in non-fiction about South America."

"No more Bushmen?" Barton, Sr., asked.

"No, Bart says he thinks the public is getting tired of Bushmen. He says he only gives Bushmen another three months and then—poo—you won't be able to *give* the books away." Bob asked what Alton thought. "Well, Alton is reading fiction now, you know. He thinks the public is getting tired of novels about murder and sex and funny war experiences. Alt thinks they're about ready for some novels about ministers. He said to one of the writers that Scribbley's publishes, 'Why don't you do a novel about a minister?' he said. And the man said he thought it was a good idea."

There was a long, comfortable silence.

There was no doubt about it. *How* the Bensons did it, Bob still didn't know. But they did do it. With absolute unconsciousness and with absolute accuracy, they were able to predict future trends in fashion. It was marvelous. It was uncanny. It—

Kitty lifted her lovely head and looked at Bob through the long, silken skein of hair, then brushed it aside. "Do you ever have any money?" she asked. It was like the sound of small silver bells, her voice. Where, compared to this, were the flat Long Island vocable of, say, Noreen? Nowhere at all.

"Why, Kitty Benson, what a question," her mother said, reaching out her glass for Bentley to refill. "Poor Peter Martens, just to think—a little more, Bentley, don't think you're going to drink what's left, young man."

"Because if you ever have any money," said the voice like the Horns of Elfland. "We could go out somewhere together. Some boys don't ever have any money," it concluded, with infinitely loving melancholy.

"I'm going to have some money," Bob said at once. "Absolutely. Uh—when could—"

She smiled an absolute enchantment of a smile. "Not tonight," she said, "because I have a date. And not tomorrow night, because I have a date. But the day after tomorrow night, because then I don't have a date."

A little voice in one corner of Bob's mind said, "This girl has a brain about the size of a small split pea; you know that, don't you?" And another voice, much less little, in the opposite corner, shrieked, "Who *cares?* Who *cares?*" Furthermore, Noreen had made a faint but definite beginning on an extra chin, and her bosom tended (unless artfully and artificially supported) to droop. Neither was true of Kitty at all, at all.

"The day after tomorrow night, then," he said. "It's a date."

All that night he wrestled with his angel. "You can't expose these people to the sordid glare of modern commerce," the angel said, throwing him with a half-nelson. "They'd wither and die. Look at the dodo—look at the buffalo. Will you *look?*" "*You* look," growled Bob, breaking the hold, and seizing the angel in a scissors-lock. "I'm not going to let any damned account executives get their chicken-plucking hands on the Bensons. It'll all be done through me, see? Through *me!*" And with that he pinned the angel's shoulders to the mat. "And besides," he said, clenching his teeth, "I need the money . . ."

Next morning he called up his agent. "Here's just a few samples to toss Mr. Phillips Anhalt's way," he said grandiosely. "Write 'em down. Soupbowl haircuts for men. *That's* what I said. They can get a sunlamp treatment for the backs of their necks in the barber-shops. Listen. Women will stencil stars on their toe-nails with nail polish. Kate Greenaway style dresses for women are going to come in. Huh? Well, you bet your butt that Anhalt will know what Kate Greenaway means. Also, what smart women will wear will be madras kerchiefs tied up in the old West Indian way. This is very complicated, so I guess they'll have to be pre-folded and pre-stitched. Silks and cottons. . . . You writing this down? Okay.

"Teen-agers will wear, summer-time, I mean, they'll wear shorts made out of cut-down blue jeans. And sandals

made out of cut-down sneakers. No shirts or undershirts
—barechested, and—What? *NO*, for cry-sake, just the
boys!"

And he gave Stuart the rest of it, books and all, and
he demanded and got an advance. Next day Stuart reported that Anhalt reported that Mac Ian was quite ex-
cited. Mac had said—did Bob know what Phil said Mac
said? Well, Mac said, "Let's not spoil the ship for a
penny's worth of tar, Phil."

Bob demanded and received another advance. When
Noreen called, he was brusque.

The late morning of his date-day he called to confirm
it. That is, he tried to. The operator said that she was
sorry, but that number had been disconnected. He made
it up to the Bronx by taxi. The house was empty. It was
not only empty of people, it was empty of everything.
The wallpaper had been left, but that was all.

Many years earlier, about the time of his first cigarette,
Bob had been led by a friend in the dead of night (say,
half-past ten) along a quiet suburban street, pledged to
confidence by the most frightful vows. Propped against
the wall of a garage was a ladder—it did not go all the
way to the roof: Bob and friend had pulled themselves
up with effort which, in another context, would have won
the full approval of their gym teacher. The roof made an
excellent post to observe the going-to-bed preparations
of a young woman who had seemingly never learned
that window shades could be pulled down. Suddenly
lights went on in another house, illuminating the roof of
the garage; the young woman had seen the two and
yelled; and Bob, holding onto the parapet with sweating
hands and reaching for the ladder with sweating feet,
had discovered that the ladder was no longer there. . . .

He felt the same way now.

Besides feeling stunned, incredulous, and panicky, he also felt annoyed. This was because he acutely realized that he was acting out an old moving picture scene. The scene would have been close to the (film) realities had he been wearing a tattered uniform, and in a way he wanted to giggle, and in a way he wanted to cry. Only through obligation to the script did he carry the farce farther: wandering in and out of empty rooms, calling out names, asking if anyone was there.

No one was. And there was no notes or messages, not even *Croatan* carved on a doorpost. Once, in the gathering shadows, he though he heard a noise, and he whirled around, half-expecting to see an enfeebled Mr. Benson with a bacon-fat lamp in one hand, or an elderly Negro, perhaps, who would say, tearfully, "Marse Bob, dem Yankees done burn all de cotton . . ." But there was nothing.

He trod the stairs to the next house and addressed inquiries to an old lady in a rocking-chair. "Well, I'm sure that *I* don't know," she said, in a paper-thin and fretful voice. "I saw them, all dressed up, getting into the car, and I said, 'Why, where are you all *going*, Hazel?' ("Hazel?" "Hazel Benson. I thought you said you *knew* them, young man?" "Oh, yes. Yes, of course. Please go on.") Well, I said, 'Where are you all *going*, Hazel?' And she said, 'It's time for a change, Mrs. Machen.' And they all laughed and they waved and they drove away. And then some men came and packed everything up and took it away in trucks. Well! 'Where did they all *go*?' I asked them. 'Where did they all *go*?' But do you think they'd have the common decency to *tell* me, after I've lived here for fifty-four years? Not-a-word. Oh—"

Feeling himself infinitely cunning, Bob said, offhandedly, "Yes, I know just the outfit you mean. O'Brien Movers."

"I do *not* mean O'Brien Movers. Whatever gave you such an idea? It was the Seven Sebastian Sisters."

And this was the most that Bob Rosen could learn. Inquiries at other houses either drew blanks or produced such probably significant items as, "Kitty said, 'Here are your curlers, because I won't need them anymore'"; "Yes, just the other day I was talking to Bart, Senior, and he said, 'You know, you don't realize that you're in a rut until you have to look up to see the sky.' Well, those Bensons always talked a little crazy, and so I thought nothing of it, until—"; and, "I said to Bentley, 'Vipe, how about tomorrow we go over to Williamsbridge and pass the chicks there in review?' and he said, 'No, Vipe, I can't make the scene tomorrow, my ancients put another poster on the billboard.' So I said, 'Ay-las,' and next thing I know—"

"His who did what?"

"Fellow, you don't wot this Viper talk one note, do you? His *family*, see, they had made other plans. They really cut loose, didn't they?"

They really did. So there Bob was, neat and trim and sweet-smelling, and nowhere to go, and with a pocketful of money. He looked around the tree-lined street and two blocks away, on the corner, he saw a neon sign. *Harry's*, it flashed (green). *Bar and Grill* (red).

"Where's Harry?" he asked the middle-aged woman behind the bar.

"Lodge meeting," she said. "He'll be back soon. They aren't doing any labor tonight, just business. Waddle ya have?"

"A ball of Bushmill," he said. He wondered where he had heard that, last. It was cool in the bar. And then he remembered, and then he shuddered.

"Oh, that's bad," Stuart Emmanuel moaned. "That

sounds very bad . . . And you shouldn't've gone to the moving van people yourself. Now you probably muddied the waters."

Bob hung his head. His efforts to extract information from the Seven Sebastian Sisters—apparently they were septuplets, and all had gray mustaches—had certainly failed wretchedly. And he kept seeing Kitty Benson's face, framed in her golden hair like a sun-lit nimbus, kept hearing Kitty Benson's golden voice.

"Well," Stuart said, "I'll do my damndest." And no doubt he did, but it wasn't enough. He was forced to come clean with Anhalt. And Anhalt, after puttering around, his sweet smile more baffled than ever, told Mac everything. Mac put the entire *force majeure* of the T. Oscar Rutherford organization behind the search. And they came up with two items.

Item. The Seven Sebastian Sisters had no other address than the one on Purchase Place, and all the furniture was in their fireproof warehouse, with two years' storage paid in advance.

Item. The owner of the house on Purchase Place said, "I told them I'd had an offer to buy the house, but I wouldn't, if they'd agree to a rent increase. And the next thing I knew, the keys came in the mail."

Little and Harpey, as well as Scribbley's Sons, reported only that Alt and Bart, Junior, had said that they were leaving, but hadn't said where they were going.

"Maybe they've gone on a trip somewhere," Stuart suggested. "Maybe they'll come back before long. Anhalt has ears in all the publishing houses, maybe he'll hear something."

But before Anhalt heard anything, Mac decided that there was no longer anything to hear. "I wash my hands of it all," he declared. "It's a wild goose chase. . Where

did you ever pick up this crackpot idea in the first place?"
And Phillips Anhalt's smile faded away. Weeks passed,
and months.

But Bob Rosen has never abandoned hope. He has
checked with the Board of Education about Bentley's
records, to see if they know anything about a transcript
or transfer. He has haunted Nassau Street, bothering—
in particular—dealers specializing in Pseudo-Arabian air
mail issues, in hopes that Mr. Benson has made his
whereabouts known to them. He had hocked his watch
to buy hamburgers and pizzas for the Vipers, and innumerable Scotches on innumerable rocks for the trim
young men and the girls fresh out of Bennington who
staff the offices of our leading publishers. He—

In short, he has taken up the search of Peter Martens
(Old Pete, Sneaky Pete). He is looking for the sources
of the Nile. Has he *ever* found *anything?* Well, yes, as
a matter of fact, he has.

The strange nature of cyclical coincidences has been
summed up, somewhere, in the classical remark that one
can go for years without seeing a one-legged man wearing a baseball cap; and then, in a single afternoon, one
will see three of them. So it happened with Bob Rosen.

One day, feeling dull and heavy, and finding that the
elfin notes of Kitty Benson's voice seemed to be growing
fainter in his mind, Bob called up her old landlord.

"No," said the old landlord, "I never heard another
word from them. And I'll tell you who else I never heard
from, either. The fellow who offered to buy the house.
He never came around and when I called his office, he
just laughed at me. Fine way to do business."

"What's his name?" Bob asked, listlessly.

"Funny name," said the old landlord. "E. Peters Shad-
wall? Something like that. The Hell with him, anyway."

Bob tore his rooms apart looking for the card with the perforated top edge which Shadwell had—it seemed so very long ago—torn off his little book and given him. Also, it struck him, neither could he find the piece of paper on which he had scribbled Old Martens' last message, with the Bensons' name and street on it. He fumbled through the Yellow Book, but couldn't seem to locate the proper category for the mantisman's business. And he gave up on the regular directory, what with Shad, Shadd, -wel, -well, -welle, etc.

He would, he decided, go and ask Stuart Emmanuel. The dapper little agent had taken the loss of the Bensons so hard ("It was a beauty of a deal," he'd all but wept) that he might also advance a small sum of money for the sake of the Quest. Bob was in the upper East 40s when he passed a bar where he had once taken Noreen for cocktails—a mistake, for it had advanced her already expensive tastes another notch—and this reminded him that he had not heard from her in some time. He was trying to calculate just how much time, and if he ought to do something about it, when he saw the third one-legged man in the baseball cap.

That is to say, speaking nonmetaphorically, he had turned to cross a street in the middle of a block, and was halted by the absence of any gap between the two vehicles (part of a traffic jam caused by a long-unclosed incision in the street) directly in front of him. Reading from right to left, the vehicles consisted of an Eleanor-blue truck reading *Grandma Goldberg's Yum-Yum Borsht,* and an Obscene-pink Jaguar containing T. Pettys Shadwell and Noreen.

It was the Moment of the Shock of Recognition. He understood everything.

Without his making a sound, they turned together and

saw him, mouth open, everything written on his face. And they knew that he knew.

"Why, Bob," said Noreen. "Ah, Rosen," said Shadwell. "I'm sorry that we weren't able to have you at the *wed*ding," she said. "But everything happened so *quickly*. Pete just swept me off my feet."

Bob said, "I'll bet."

She said, "Don't be bitter"—seeing that he was, and enjoying it. Horns sounded, voices cursed, but the line of cars didn't move.

"You did it," Bob said, coming close. Shadwell's hands left the wheel and came together at his chest, fingers down. "*You* saw that crisp green money he left and you saw his card and got in touch with him and *you* came in and took the note and—*Where are they?*" he shouted, taking hold of the small car and shaking it. "I don't give a damn about the money, just tell me where they are! Just let me see the girl!"

But T. Pettys Shadwell just laughed and laughed, his voice like the whisper of the wind in the dry leaves. "Why, *Bob*," said Noreen, bugging her eyes and flashing her large, coarse gems, and giving the scene all she had, "why, Bob, was there a *girl?* You never told *me*."

Bob abandoned his anger, disclaimed all interest in the commercial aspect of the Bensons, offered to execute bonds and sign papers in blood, if only he were allowed to see Kitty. Shadwell, fingering his tiny carat of a mustache, shrugged. "Write the girl a letter," he said, smirking. "I assure you, all mail will be forwarded." And then the traffic jam broke and the Jag zoomed off, Noreen's scarlet lips pursed in blowing a kiss.

"Write?" Why, bless you, of course Bob wrote. Every day and often twice a day for weeks. But never a reply did he get. And on realizing that his letters prob-

ably went no farther than Noreen (Mrs. T. Pettys) Shadwell, who doubtless gloated and sneered in the midst of
her luxury, he fell into despair, and ceased. Where is
Kitty of the heart-shaped face, Kitty of the light-gold
hair, Kitty of the elfin voice? Where are her mother and
father and her three brothers? Where now are the sources
of the Nile? Ah, where?

So there you are. One can hardly suppose that Shadwell has perforce kidnapped the entire Benson family,
but the fact is that they have disappeared almost entirely without trace, and the slight trace which remains
leads directly to and only to the door of T. Pettys Shadwell Associates, Market Research Advisors. Has he
whisked them all away to some sylvan retreat in the
remote recesses of the Great Smoky Mountains? Are they
even now pursuing their prophetic ways in one of the
ever-burgeoning, endlessly proliferating suburbs of the
City of the Angels? Or has he, with genius disabolical,
located them so near to hand that far-sighted vision must
needs forever miss them?

In deepest Brooklyn, perhaps, amongst whose labyrinthine ways an army of surveyors could scare find their
own stakes?—or in fathomless Queens, red brick and
yellow brick, world without end, where the questing
heart grows sick and faint?

Rosen does not know, but he has not ceased to care.
He writes to live, but he lives to look, now selling, now
searching, famine succeeding feast, but hope never failing.

Phillips Anhalt, however, has not continued so successfully. He has not Bob's hopes. Anhalt continues, it is
true, with the T. Oscar Rutherford people, but no longer
has his corner office, or any private office at all. Anhalt

failed: Anhalt now has a desk in the bullpen with the other failures and the new apprentices.

And while Bob ceaselessly searches the streets—for who knows in which place he may find the springs bubbling and welling?—and while Anhalt drinks bitter tea and toils like a slave in a salt mine, that swine, that cad, that most despicable of living men, T. Pettys Shadwell, has three full floors in a new building of steel, aluminum, and blue-green glass a block from the Cathedral; he has a box at the Met, a house in Bucks County, a place on the Vineyard, an apartment in Beekman Place, a Caddy, a Bentley, *two* Jaguars, a yacht that sleeps ten, and one of the choicest small (but ever-growing) collection of Renoirs in private hands today. . . .